WESTCOUNTR
RESTL

"Oh, come you from earth?" she said,
"Or come you from the skye?"
"Oh, I am from yonder churchyard,
Where my crumbling relicks lie."

Anon.

"Some annoyance may be experienced from the
psychic portion of the subjects, which popular
language dignifies with the name of ghosts."

M. R. James:
Lost Hearts.

"...A little ere the mightiest Julius fell,
The graves stood tenantless, and the sheeted dead
Did squeak and gibber in the Roman streets;"

William Shakespeare:
Hamlet, Act One, Scene One.

WESTCOUNTRY STORIES OF THE RESTLESS DEAD

LAURENCE GREEN

MOORHEN PUBLISHING LLP

First published in Great Britain in 2008 by
Moorhen Publishing LLP
1 Hazelwood Close, Windmill Hill, Brixham, Devon, TQ5 9SE
www.moorhenpublishing.co.uk

Distributed by Laurence Green
8 Holly Villas, Ashprington, Totnes, TQ9 7UU
Tel: +44 (0) 1803 732437
Email: kcgreen@supanet.com

A CIP catalogue record for this book is available
from the British Library.

ISBN   978-1-905856-04-6

Cover design by Deep Red Designs
using an original drawing by Tom Green
Printed and bound in Great Britain by
SRP Limited, Exeter, Devon

Dedication

This book is dedicated to
Jamie M., Toby R., Chris D. and James W.:
very special KEVICC students.

Contents

Mr. Hendra's Charabanc..7
A Sense of Loss 9
Danse Macabre 19
The Old A38 27
Room Number 4 35
Tom Tucker 44
Operation Paper Tiger...54
Veyther 68
Babbacombe Lee 78
Floreat Totnesia 90
Private Angove 100
Young Harry 112
Sir Cloudesley...120
Vade mecum 127
Cutty Dyer 136
Clouds Hill..143
Parcere Subjectis...153
An Adventure...162
Mrs Carey-Carew...171
It wasn't William… 181
Miss Wilberforce 194
Afterword...202
About Laurence Green..224

Mr. Hendra's Charabanc

The cold white moon shone through the leafless branches of the oak as the clock, high in the tower of Cornworthy church, struck midnight. The sound jarred round the square where Mr Hendra's charabanc idled noisily in the shadow of the schoolhouse wall, lamps lit and polished steel dully gleaming. Once again it was November 2nd and time for the annual excursion. Mr Hendra, a tall man dressed in a heavy greatcoat and muffler, impatiently tapped the brim of his shiny bowler hat.

"'Tis time to be off, my handsomes," he called across the square in a high voice which rose above the burble of the engine. A few shadowy shapes emerged from the dark corners of the square and hesitantly climbed into the swaying conveyance to join the indistinct figures sitting uncertainly on the bench seats which rose behind the driver to the rounded rump of coachwork overhanging the rear wheels. Although the vehicle was open, with seats exposed to the dark sky, none of the passengers wore coat or jacket. Nor did they talk or laugh; each sat self-contained in a seat isolated from the others.

Mr Hendra noisily found first gear, took off the handbrake and let in the clutch. The charabanc moved jerkily forward and rolled down the hill with the blare of exhaust, stopping from time to time to pick up small knots of people who waited in the shadows. George Arscott, half his head missing where a horse had kicked him, clambered aboard, as did Mary Ellis, dark rings round her eyes and a tightly wrapped still bundle in her arms. At the bottom of the village a soldier climbed up into his seat, his khaki tunic ripped open to show white ribs protruding from a dark mass of mangled flesh.

With a clash of gears and a roar of exhaust, the charabanc climbed the hill towards the white moon which hung just over the hedge. As it did so its outline wavered and became indistinct, the passengers growing faint and opaque. Only the thin figure of Mr Hendra remained solid for a moment before the whole assemblage faded into the dark sky, leaving behind in the lane the momentary roar of the motor to fade into the void.

A Sense of Loss

As the car followed the ribbon of road unreeling towards the low clouds that overhung the moor, Hugh felt incredibly alone even as Helen sat beside him looking out of the windscreen at the rising of the land. Lush green fields enclosed by leafy hedges gave way to open stretches of wide moorland, bent thorn trees and distant piles of rough granite, all glimpsed in the fading evening light. Neither person spoke; the loss of their son Tom lay like a fog in the car. Only that morning he had left for Australia and a new life after college. Of course they would see him again, but he would be changed by the experiences that awaited him.

It was Helen who at last broke the silence. "I think I can see the lights of Bolventor ahead," she said quietly. On the crest of a hill in front of them a solitary light gleamed from a cluster of dark buildings that seemed to huddle beneath the gusts of fitful wind which pressed down on them from a vast empty sky. It was a cold light to welcome them to the remote

Jamaica Inn where they had phoned ahead to spend the night.

Hugh steered the car off the divided ribbon of the A30 onto a side road that led up the slope to the small village of Bolventor. They passed a few cottages before turning into the car park that lay beside the inn. As he helped Helen out of the car Hugh realised that the silence was almost absolute; apart from the occasional swish of tyres from the trunk road below the inn and the distant cry of a few night birds only the hollow blasts of wind could be heard. The couple walked round the side of the building towards the light perched atop a gibbet-like structure that framed the dark sign proclaiming the "Jamaica Inn". Arm in arm they walked across the granite cobbles made slick by the low mist that hung over the moor. Behind the thick curtains of the small-paned windows could be heard the muffled voices and the indistinct drone of conversations.

Hugh opened the massive door and ushered Helen into the warm fug of the inn. A few people looked up as they entered and nodded in a friendly way before returning to their conversations or games of euchre. A log fire burned to the right of the low beamed room behind tables and low backed settles. Hugh approached the bar and order two pints of Tinners' which he carried over to Helen who sat near the fire staring at the sparks rising into the wide chimney.

"I reckon that Tom must be in the air by now. It will almost be summer when he arrives in Sydney. I must say that I envy him two summers in a row," he said.

"I'm sorry to be so quiet," replied Helen. "We just have to get used to not having him around all the time. I know that he wasn't the tidiest person in the world but I'm even going to miss the mess he made."

The couple sat in silence feeling the hollow sense of loss which they would share for some considerable time to come. Hugh raised his eyes to the barman who stood politely in front of him. "Mr and Mrs Drake, your room is ready for you and supper is served after seven o'clock," he said, his soft Australian drawl contrasting with the westcountry burr of the conversations surrounding them.

Hugh and Helen walked past the bar into Reception. On the walls were a collection of old prints and, opposite a stuffed pheasant in a glass case, Hugh's attention was held by a small framed photograph in black and white of a young man wearing an overcoat and round glasses who looked down with a sardonic and slightly bemused air, his mouth twisted into a forced smile. Under the photograph was a very curious typed inscription to the effect that the young man portrayed, Percival

Fotherington-Casters-Smythe, born at the Jamaica Inn on January 19th 1921, had inexplicably vanished on Bodmin Moor during an elaborate game of hide and seek on his twenty-eighth birthday on January 19th 1949. He was presumed dead and mourned by all his friends in Britain and Australia.

"How awful," said Helen. "And how terrible for his family. To think that the photo was taken on the very day of his death."

"I suppose that he must have died out on the moor, possibly in a bog or down a ravine," replied Hugh. "I really don't want to think about it any more. It reminds me of the miles of moorland surrounding us, quite a howling wilderness in the middle of winter. Come on up the stairs and look at our room, Helen."

Together they climbed the uneven stairs which twisted up to the low ceilinged bedrooms of the old granite building. They were delighted by their room which combined modern comfort with the ancient charm of the inn. When they opened the curtains and the small latticed casement window they were enchanted by the view of the moor. The moon had risen over a tor that lay due north of the inn; the road lay invisible in the dead ground before the moor rose gently towards the tumbled mass of granite on the skyline. Wispy clouds were blown across the wide sky, the cloud shadows briefly darkening expanses of rough ground before moving on. Hugh and Helen felt their spirits lift for the first time that day. The aching gloom that had enfolded them since they had left their home in Devon was beginning to clear like the dark clouds that scudded before the wind just outside their window.

As the booming wind subsided in the hollow sky Hugh and Helen made ready for bed. They pulled back the crisp sheets and slid drowsily into the cool bed.

"Goodnight, darling," murmured Helen as sleep invaded her tired body.

Several hours later Hugh came slowly awake. Outside the granite walls of their bedroom all was still. He turned over to see a tall man standing in the corner of the room by the window. The man stood quietly looking towards Hugh, the moonlight glinting on his round glasses. He wore a long dark overcoat and a woollen scarf wound round his throat. In one hand he held a tweed cap and in the other a pair of leather gloves. Hugh did not feel threatened or frightened in any way. He could see that the expression on the pale face was earnest and anxious. Hugh did not speak or move; he said in his mind: "Can I help you in some way, Percy?"

A faint smile crossed the figure's face and he swiftly transferred his gloves to the left hand, raising the right hand slowly towards the window to point in the direction of the tor that Hugh knew lay a mile away across the moor. A look of entreaty crossed the tall man's face as his outline started to fade as the energy left him. Soon there was no trace in the corner of the room that a visitor had been there, only a feeling of peace and resolve. Glad that his wife still slumbered at his side, Hugh turned over and fell back to sleep almost immediately.

Dawn came with birdsong and shafts of brilliant sunshine. Hugh and Helen awoke refreshed and dressed hurriedly so as not to miss breakfast. They sat by a window with a clear view of the tor on the northern skyline and enjoyed an excellent breakfast.

"Hugh darling, last night I kept dreaming about that poor Percy who disappeared on the moor. In my dream he was talking to Tom about something or other; I never worked out what he was on about. In the end he went away and that was it," she said, looking intently at Hugh.

"Let's walk up to that tor on the skyline after breakfast. Perhaps that's where he vanished," he replied with a chuckle. "It's a lovely morning and we need to clear a few cobwebs out of our heads."

"Don't be unkind. You know what's on our minds and I suppose we must try not to get too morose," said Helen.

"I'm sorry. Tom will be in Singapore by now and very glad to get off the wretched plane for a while. He must be quite excited by the thought of his new life on the sheep station in New South Wales," said Hugh with an enthusiasm that he knew was mainly manufactured.

A few minutes later the couple left the inn, drove under the A30 and parked their car in front of the abandoned Bolventor church. Yards away from the swish of traffic, they opened the rusty black gates and walked into the mossy churchyard. Rows of slate and granite marked the quiet resting places of generations of Sleeps, Hoskens and Hoopers, but of the Fotherington-Casters-Smythes there was no sign. Hugh noticed that the Victorian church was for sale, its roof marred by slipping slates and its windows blank with hardboard. Despite the warmth of the sun he shivered; the church, cut off from the rest of the village by the new trunk road could not even now be called the ghost of a church.

Hugh and Helen walked up the rough track which rose between uneven granite walls to the open moorland behind a low farm that seemed to crouch on the valley's side. Particles of granite crunched beneath their feet as they looked up at the tumbled tor in front of them. Now thoroughly warmed, they strode upwards through the short grass feeling the sun's rays on their shoulders.

"Hugh, there's someone standing beside the tor. I didn't see him there a minute ago," said Helen a little breathlessly.

Hugh raised his head and saw a tall figure silhouetted against the sky, the long overcoat stirring in a slight breeze. Apart from the movement of the coat the figure was motionless, the glare of the sun now glinting from round glasses. Hugh could clearly see the somewhat old fashioned cap and leather gloves as well as the long woollen scarf wound tightly around the neck.

"He must be so hot after the climb," exclaimed Helen. As she spoke a second figure seemed to rise out of the turf beside the tall man, a slight female form muffled in a grey gabardine mackintosh. Only her dark hair moved in the breeze that neither Hugh nor Helen felt in the still autumn morning.

Slowly the tall man raised his right arm to point towards the south-eastern horizon where the silver waters of the Tamar glistened far out of sight. The two forms began to fade away, the man's smile being the last impression to go.

"Goodbye Percy," Hugh found himself murmuring. Helen, understanding at last, held his arm tightly as they turned and walked down the slope of the track.

Hugh and Helen enjoyed the few days of holiday left to them at the Jamaica Inn. They slept and ate well, walked on the moor and researched the history of the inn and the surrounding area. Of the vanished Percival and his family they found no reference anywhere. On the third day of their stay a phone message reassured them that their son Tom had arrived safely in the antipodes and was making his way across country to the sheep station which was to become his home for at least the next year. So Hugh and Helen packed up, settled the bill and left for home. They drove a little reluctantly away from the inn and downhill off the moor to arrive home to their snug little cottage in a couple of short hours.

A few weeks later the first thick letter arrived from Tom at the Waggeroo Sheep Station in Bongalong, New South Wales. As Hugh opened it he felt a strange tingling in his fingers. Tom wrote that he found the place to his liking, the work was long and hard and the company friendly and good. He was glad that he had gone there although, of course, he missed his parents and his home. Only one sadness clouded the life of the station; the recent death of the old man who had owned and run the spread since the 1950s.

"…and here's an extraordinary coincidence," wrote Tom Drake.

"The old man came originally from Cornwall; he was born at the Jamaica Inn in 1921. When the war began he volunteered for the Army and was eventually sent to the Western Desert to fight Rommel's army alongside a Division of the Australian Army. He survived the war and came home to his family on Bodmin Moor. He never settled down and fell in love with a girl from one of the moorland farms. Unfortunately the girl's father owed the old man's father rather a lot of money and the families were no longer on speaking terms. When the love affair was discovered there was hell to pay; the old man was disinherited and virtually thrown out. As he turned twenty-eight a party was put on for him at the Jamaica Inn as if nothing had happened, to keep up appearances as much as anything.

It was on that January day that the old man faked his disappearance and ran away to Australia with his intended. The family was left to wonder if he had died as a result of an accident on the moor or if he had committed suicide. They never found out what had really happened and he never let them know, such was his anger at their hard-hearted attitude. He did very well in New South Wales and became quite a wealthy man running the sheep station. His wife died a couple of years ago and he followed her on January 19th, soon after I arrived here. By the way, his name was Percy Smythe …

Danse Macabre

Endicott House was a late Victorian pile with very little about its architecture to recommend it. It squatted solidly at the top of a hill on the edge of the town, its one good facade facing over sloping lawns towards an overgrown shrubbery which hid it from the town. The other three sides of the house were irregular and functional, festooned with fire escapes and encumbered with all the extensions required by a successful sixth - form college. Tall trees surrounded the house, hiding it from the road below and giving it the feeling of isolation from the sprawling school buildings at the foot of the hill.

Becoming a sixth former involved not only achieving the requisite GCSE grades but also climbing the hill and leaving behind the heaving masses at the foot of the slope. Susanna Jenken and Rose Tucker had successfully made the transition to the rarefied ambience of Endicott House and were working hard for their A levels. Both had a great interest in photography; both were working towards an A grade in the subject. Each had fully mastered the arcane art of developing her own negatives in the dark room which was situated not far from the back door of the house.

Mrs Poe, the Deputy Principal with special responsibility for the Sixth Form, was sitting at her desk in her panelled study on the ground floor. She was rarely able to catch up with her paperwork and treasured the closed door and the quiet phone. She completed a report on one of the Oxbridge potentials and glanced out of the window at the back drive. All was quiet, even the purposeful hum of work seemed far away. The church clock across the valley struck twelve and the far off siren of an ambulance could barely be heard.

A shrill scream split the air, followed by another. A door slammed and panicked footsteps raced down the corridor towards Mrs Poe's door. Shrieks and sobs accompanied the flight. Mrs Poe stood up and walked over to open the study door.

"What on earth is going on?" she said in as stern a voice as she could muster. Two shaking girls stood in front of her sobbing uncontrollably. "You'd better come in and sit down," she said, visibly shaken.

It took at least five minutes for Susanna and Rose to gain control of themselves. They sat on two low chairs in front of Mrs Poe's desk, pale and dishevelled; quite unlike their usual well groomed selves. Rose spoke first:

"It's horrible Mrs Poe! It's just a shape, a woman in old -fashioned clothes. But it wasn't there when I took the photo. It just appeared from nowhere on the print.... Oh, my God..." She dissolved into sobs as the tears ran down her cheeks.

Susanna looked up at Mrs Poe with red rimmed eyes, her long hair in strings across her face.

"It can't be a trick, it's too real! I don't ever want to look at it again," she said, running her fingers through her hair.

"What figure? What woman? Please start at the beginning," said Mrs Poe patiently.

She had a feeling that the girls were not wasting her time and that they desperately needed her help. Besides, she was very curious as to what had frightened two intelligent and sensible girls.

Gradually she pieced the story together. Earlier in the day the two girls had gone up to a passage on the second floor in what had once been the servants' quarters. Rose had opened the back of the camera and put a new film carefully into it, winding on and opening the shutter twice before taking photos of the trees at odd angles from the upper windows. Pleased with their choice of subject matter, the girls had developed the passage film in the dark room under the red light that burned close to the ceiling. The two

21

first pictures should have been blank, showing only the wall of the corridor with its few cracks and irregularities. But what emerged on the second blank exposure was a tall and hazy female figure in what appeared to be a long dress. As the shape became clearer the shape of a slim waist could clearly be seen, then two upraised arms enveloped in some flimsy material. Finally the shape of a head became apparent with two glowing spots where the eyes should be. The figure seemed to stand sideways to the camera with a long scarf trailing off the shoulder on the left hand side. The feet were invisible because they were covered by the folds of the long dress. At this point Susanna screamed and dropped the wet print on the bench. Both girls had run out of the dark room in hysterics leaving the door open and the prints behind them. Finally Mrs Poe succeeded in calming the girls and suggested that, when they had fully recovered, they go back up to the passage and look at marks on the wall, patterns in the wallpaper, or trailing curtains which could have been responsible for the human shape in their photograph. Susanna and Rose left the office looking subdued and slightly pale. They walked back along the corridor to retrieve the prints that they had left so hurriedly in the dark room. Quickly Rose put them in an envelope and placed them in her locker, turning her back on them to go down to the library to research early twentieth century dancers for an Independent Studies essay that was due in a couple of days' time.

A few days later, on a hazy winter afternoon, the two girls ventured back upstairs to the passage under the eaves where they had taken the photos which had frightened them so badly. They felt ashamed of their fear and had convinced themselves that there was, after all, a rational explanation for the figure on the print. The wind blew softly round the upper storey of Endicott House as they examined the irregular plaster of the wall and the horrible striped curtains that bordered the small windows that looked out onto the bare and twisted upper branches of dreary wellingtonia and scots pines. They saw nothing that faintly resembled a draped female shape, even though they tipped the shades on the lights to reflect different intensities of light onto the walls and ceiling of the passage. They felt removed from the rest of the college and were glad that they still had over twenty minutes before English Literature, the last class of the day.

Susanna noticed that Rose had moved to the far end of the passage and that she had a dreamy look on her face. Rose closed her eyes and slowly raised her arms to the ceiling, gently pirouetting on her toes as she glided towards Susanna.

"Don't be silly, Rose. Cut it out, you're frightening me..." called Susanna as Rose swept towards her on her toes, arms outstretched, bending backwards from the waist. As she came near to Susanna, Rose opened her eyes, showing only the white orbs behind fluttering lashes.

"Rose!" shrieked Susanna.

"Laisse-moi tranquille, pour l'amour de Dieu. Je suis en train de danser. Laisse-moi, je t'en prie!" growled Rose in a voice totally unlike her own, the French accent overlaid with an American intonation. As Susanna pressed her back against the wall with her hands to her face as if to blot out the sight of her friend behaving in such a bizarre way, Rose crumpled onto the worn carpet of the passage. Her eyes closed and opened again as she appeared to regain consciousness.

"Rose, what were you playing at? You scared me badly. Who were you?" Susanna asked plaintively. Rose lay on the carpet in a state of pale confusion.

"I feel as if all the energy has been sucked out of me. Did I faint? What really happened?" asked Rose faintly. "I was myself, but someone called I D was with me."

Susanna knew that Rose did not speak French and wondered why she had spoken in that weird voice. She had to take Rose away from this remote part of the house and find the answers at a later time.

A couple of days later the two girls were sitting in front of a computer in the Endicott Library. Rose was rather quiet, still obviously shaken by her experience. Neither girl had mentioned what had happened to them to anyone. They had decided to research the history of Endicott House in order to find out if any foreign dancer had ever visited the building. After half an hour they were closer to the truth than they had thought possible.

Mrs Poe was sitting at her desk writing a report on a student who hardly seemed to attend any of his classes. She heard the two girls rapidly approach and rap on her door.

"Come in," she called out. The girls looked a little flushed as they came into her study. They sat down breathlessly and each started to talk at the same time.

"Mrs Poe, we have found an explanation for the figure on the print," said Susanna. "This house was built in the late nineteenth century by the Singer family who gained their wealth from sewing machines. Paris Singer was often here with his mistress. She was an American dancer who had lived for a long time in France. When she was here she was having a growing problem with drug addiction, having lost her children who were drowned when the car they were in ran out of control backwards into a river. Her only relief was to dance. She had a tragic life and a strange death. She loved to drive fast cars along the mountainous roads of the French Riviera. One day, as her car accelerated away from her house, her long scarf caught in the spokes of the wheel of her car and broke her neck. She died instantly. Her name was Isadora Duncan..."

"Do you really think that she haunts this place? Why on earth should she?" puzzled Mrs Poe. At that point the phone rang, startling them all. Mrs Poe quickly picked up the receiver, a little impatient at the interruption. Mr Jeffries, the Principal, was calling with some good news.

"Edwina, do you remember our bid for Arts Status? Well, I'm very glad to tell you that we have been successful. I can't help feeling that we must have had a bit of help from some unexpected quarter because our bid had been accepted. Thank heavens. Now we will be able to afford to build the new dance studio on the site where the old swimming pool used to be..."

The Old A38

At last Gerald was going home. He had enjoyed the conference in Birmingham on the literary links between the Midlands and the New World, but he was keen to leave the redbrick houses and thorn hedges and return home to the deep valleys and red soil of Devon. He drove at a monotonous seventy miles an hour across the Somerset levels leaving the abrupt hills of the Mendips behind him and heading across flat fields towards the westering sun dipping into a bank of clouds. Soon he passed the King's Sedgemoor Drain and the striding figure of the willow man, arms outstretched as he too marched towards the west. He passed the yellow camel on a gradual right hand curve around Bridgwater, noticing the absence of the usual sharp celanese smell. The ground rose imperceptibly between Bridgwater and Taunton as the Quantock Hills rose to the right. Taunton approached with the frowning Blackdowns rearing in front of the motorway.

When Gerald had spotted the four trees on the skyline he knew that the Devon border was only minutes away. Taunton came brashly to meet the motorway and Gerald felt suddenly and desperately tired. He would have to turn off onto the old A38 and find a lay-by to have a quiet nap if he were going to drive safely back to his home in Devon. He turned off the M5 just after Taunton and turned onto the almost deserted A38, away from the constant swish of traffic, speeding trucks and four wheel drives. After a couple of miles of twisting and turning on the two lane road he parked in a secluded lay-by under some damp trees and, turning off his engine, slept deeply for ten minutes. He awoke refreshed, wondering for a second where he was. He stretched and saw that the dark clouds were rolling in from the west, covering the sun as it dipped towards the western horizon. Fat drops begun to spatter his windscreen as he started the engine. He pulled out and switched on the wipers as rain swept across his vision. The windscreen cleared and Gerald saw in front of him a man in a light coloured raincoat standing at the side of the road waving his right arm in the gathering gloom. Feeling a pang of anxiety, he stopped to pick him up, leaning over to open the door on the passenger's side.

"Hop in, friend. Where can I take you to?" asked Gerald, wondering why he had stopped when he never picked up strangers. This man had seemed incredibly lonely as he stood helplessly beside the deserted road. He was well dressed and seemed to pose no threat.

The man seemed to suddenly appear in the passenger's seat. One second he was standing beside the road, the next he was sitting next to Gerald.

"A few miles down the road, if you don't mind," he said staring through the windscreen in front of him. Gerald noticed that his white raincoat was bone dry and that he gave off a faint smell like a pheasant that has hung for too long in the shed. He was a man in early middle age with a curiously old fashioned air about him. He was obviously local; a faint Somerset burr in his voice made that plain. He wore a tweed suit under his belted raincoat and carried a furled black umbrella in his left hand. Although polite, he seemed remote and did not look directly at Gerald.

The car accelerated towards Wellington and the tall monument on the hill. As it passed the turning to West Buckland at Heatherton Grange the man spoke again. As he talked Gerald's gaze was drawn to the left towards the wooded hills of the frowning Blackdowns.

"A few years ago there was a terrible accident here," the man said. "A butcher's boy on a bicycle was decapitated as he turned out onto the main road. A man speeding in a Jaguar never stopped until he hit a lorry at Beam Bridge and was killed instantly. He left the headless body and the crushed bike in the middle of the road. They didn't find the head for several weeks after the accident. Eventually a policeman on a bike smelled something and found what was left of the head in the fork of a tree beside the road. They had to identify it by dental records and re-open the grave to bury it with the rest of the body."

Gerald shuddered as he noticed that the light was beginning to fade. The rain poured from a darkening sky as Gerald's passenger sat rigid beside him staring ahead through the windscreen.

"A nasty accident happened right here a few years ago. Three cars were involved in a smash when one of them overtook a Reliant Robin on a bend. Five people were killed. It took two hours to cut out the driver of the Robin. He was in three pieces. A week later a dog found his scalp in the ditch, over there," said the man tonelessly.

Gerald said nothing, gritting his teeth as he drove carefully around the bend. A lone sunbeam slanted down from a bank of dark clouds that was spreading rapidly from the horizon. He changed down to third gear on the long rise up to Chelston Roundabout.

The man spoke again: "Only last month there was a terrible accident on this hill. A sports car drove into a petrol tanker and both drivers were killed in the explosion. Both bodies were charred beyond recognition. Only the hands of the driver of the sports car were left intact gripping the wheel with the two white bones protruding from the burned flesh of the arms."

"Enough!" said Gerald. "This is where you get out! I haven't enjoyed your company and I'm taking a left at the roundabout and going back onto the motorway..."

"I wouldn't take that road today if I were you. I wish you good evening and a safe journey home. Thank you for the lift and for the company," replied the man quietly. Then, for the first time, he slowly turned and looked at Gerald who was turning into a lay-by just before the roundabout. Gerald turned impatiently and looked at him with a real feeling of irritation.

To his dying day he would never forget the man's face illuminated in the bright headlights of an oncoming car. The eyes were empty and of a milky colour, the eyebrows and hair burnt away. The nose and lips had shrivelled away from the shattered teeth which protruded at odd angles from the dislocated jaw. The ruined face held no expression; all humanity had been smashed and burned out of it a long time ago.

Gerald shouted his revulsion and flung open his door, leaping out into the wet road in a blind panic to get away from the burned mummy beside him. He shook violently and a gust of wind took him a few paces away from the car. The cold rain plastered his hair to his face and ran down his collar as he turned back towards his car in the dazzle of oncoming headlights. He saw that his door was open and, although the passenger door was shut, there was nobody sitting in the passenger's seat. Shakily he peered into the open door of his car. It was quite empty. He had to get out of the wind and lashing rain before he was soaked.

With a curse he flung himself back into the driver's seat and slammed his door shut. He kept his dome light on and looked over his shoulder to make sure that nothing crouched in the back seat. Satisfied that he was alone, he started the engine and switched off the dome light with fingers that still trembled. He pulled carefully out onto the empty road as the last sunbeam faded from the wrack of dark clouds massing from the west.

As he drove onto the roundabout he remembered the man's words warning him not to take the road back onto the motorway. Reluctantly he swung the car to the right and took the A38 in the direction of Cullompton. He began to relax as dusk gave way to night and the driving became easier. Four or five miles further on Gerald drove over a rise towards another roundabout. He decided to leave the old A38 and get back onto the motorway at last. In the bright beam of his headlights, there beside the glistening expanse of the deserted road, Gerald saw a man in a light coloured raincoat waving his right arm with a motion that was sickeningly familiar.

"No!" shouted Gerald. "Stay where you are. Get away from me!" Gritting his teeth once more he drove past the figure, his eyes drawn inexorably towards it. He had the impression of the dry coat, the raised arm, the flash of teeth and then he was past, safe to turn onto the short stretch of dual carriageway leading to the twin streams of the motorway.

When he turned, at last, onto the M5 Gerald was surprised to find the westbound lanes deserted. With a constant stream of traffic throwing up a sheet of spray to his right he drove rapidly over the border into Devon away from weird events of Somerset. More relaxed now, he turned on his radio, tuning it automatically to Radio Devon. He sped westward, the steady rhythm of his wipers combining with the warm interior of the car to relax him.

The voice from the radio intruded on his consciousness:

"Here is a newsflash. All three southbound lanes of the M5 are completely blocked by a multiple collision at the Chelston Interchange which occurred about twenty minutes ago. A man in a Vauxhall Astra is believed to have collided with a petrol tanker while joining the motorway from the Chelston Roundabout approach road. Casualties are expected to be high from the collision and the resulting fire. Ambulances and fire appliances from Taunton, Exeter and all towns in between are attending the scene of the accident. The motorway is expected to remain blocked for many hours before the fires can be brought under control and the wreckage towed away. Stay tuned and we will keep you posted."

Gerald, now only a few minutes away from his wife and his home, smiled for the first time for a long time. His smile was grim as he spoke aloud: "Thank you God and thank you too, my burned friend in the white raincoat..."

Room Number 4

The coach clattered over the Tamar into Cornwall at Polson Bridge. Almost immediately, it began to climb the hill into Launceston, the horses blowing and straining under the coachman's whip. It was a warm September day in the year 1849; the drooping trees that lined the river had not yet begun to turn. The hilly countryside lay drowsing under the afternoon sun which warmed the granite and slate houses of the ancient hilltop town as it sat under the dark ramparts of its castle.

In the coach's dark interior John Hardy sweated into his heavy woollen suit, glad that his long, staged journey from Worcester was nearly at an end. He was a small man, slightly balding with a neat moustache and a slightly foreign air about him. He knew Launceston well, having sold many pairs of excellent Worcester gloves to merchants in the town. Indeed, he counted a number of clients there as his friends, men such as John Ching and Thomas Treleaven.

Despite his relief at his imminent arrival, Hardy felt queasy and giddy. His stomach rolled in an alarming fashion as cramps gripped his intestines. He thought grimly that he must have eaten something rotten, perhaps in Exeter where he had changed coaches. He looked out of the window as the coach reached the top of the hill and swung into Okehampton Street to rattle beneath overhanging houses. Finally, with the postillion's horn tooting, the sweating horses drew the coach through the tight arch of the South Gate, past Ching's Wine Vaults, round the corner into Broad Street, to draw to a swaying, creaking halt in front of the ancient arched doorway of the White Hart Inn.

Hardy broke into a cold sweat as he was helped out of the coach. Clammily he clasped the hand of Mr Pattison, landlord of the inn. His heavy trunk with its numerous samples was passed down from the roof of the coach to be picked up from the granite pavement by a man in a green baize apron who, directed by Pattison, took it directly up to Room 4, Hardy's usual abode at the White Hart.

"I'll go directly to my room and not take supper this evening. I feel a little indisposed after my long journey and do not wish to be disturbed. I will give you further instructions in the morning," said Hardy.

Grasping the banister he climbed slowly to his room accompanied by an anxious Pattison who carried his bag.

"I bid you goodnight, Sir, and trust that you will pass a good night," he replied.

Before turning in, Hardy took off his coat and his waistcoat, sat on the side of the high bed and looked out of the window at the busy street below. He could hear faint shouts and the clatter of iron-shod wheels coming from below him. Waves of nausea and dizziness came over him as he lay, at last, on the bed, stretching full length. Then appalling pains wrenched his tired stomach and, as he drew his knees up to almost touch his chin, his bowels turned to water.

Next morning the sun shone from a cloudless sky as Hardy came a little shakily down the stairs from his room to begin the day's business. He looked a little pale but his face wore its usual determined look. In his gloved right hand he carried a small leather bag of samples and his appointment book. He was greeted in the hallway by a slightly worried Pattison.

"I trust you passed a good night and are feeling better this morning, Mr Hardy," he asked.

"Much better thank you, Mr Pattison." Hardy replied. "I will not take breakfast this morning however. And, one more thing: please do not enter my room today. I do not wish for any disturbance. I wish you a good day."

"Very well, Sir. I will instruct the maid not to make your bed today and will see that you are at no time disturbed," said Pattison, slightly mystified. He thought that Hardy must have shaved in cold water this morning, having sent the girl away with the ewer of hot water over half an hour ago. Hardy didn't look too indisposed however, apart from a pronounced pallor and dark circles under his eyes.

Hardy's day started well with an appointment with Mr Hicks at his large draper's shop in Southgate Street. He placed an order for three gross of assorted leather gloves for the winter and was in excellent spirits as he walked to the other side of the town to an appointment with Mr Hoskins. He felt light and insubstantial, no doubt as a result of not having eaten for nearly twenty-four hours. Surprisingly, he felt no hunger and refused the tea and biscuits offered by Mr Hoskins in his snug parlour behind the shop. With another substantial order in his pocket, Hardy walked up a street between large brick houses of classic proportions to emerge from the North Gate onto the wide grounds under the Castle. Turning his back on the ragged pile of the castle keep he looked over the rising countryside unfolding to the west. Above the valley of the River Kensey, small fields rose to a wooded horizon. Hardy felt, with some sadness, that he would never look at this view again, would never return to Launceston. He felt that, somehow, his business here was nearly done and that a chapter was finally closing for him.

In the meantime, however, he had one more call to make. He would visit his old friend John Ching, a man of much influence in the town and a very good customer. If only Hardy could summon up a little energy and shake off the growing feeling of detachment that was invading his limbs. One more call to make having come so far; surely he could manage that much and finish the day's work with an outstandingly good result for the firm in Worcester that had always treated him so well and had always placed so much confidence in him.

Wearily he stood outside the front door of the Ching house in Broad Street, separated from the White Hart by only a stone bank building. He pulled the handle for the bell, hearing the echoes fade into the chambers of the house. A maid opened the door. She noticed a small man with what she could only describe later as a "faded" appearance. She motioned him in, taking his hat and stick, before offering him a seat in the front room. He sat lightly down, sighing quietly as his limbs relaxed into the leather chair.

John Ching came into the room. He was shocked by the appearance of his friend and colleague. As Hardy rose to shake his hand Ching noticed that he had aged noticeably since last he saw him. He thought that Hardy was thin and that he had a waxy complexion; his hand was cold and his eye unnaturally bright and staring.

"Please sit down my dear fellow," said Ching. "I am glad to see you again and ready to do business. Winter draws on and with it the need for a quantity of your excellent Worcester gloves. I trust that you are in good health after your long and tedious journey from the Midlands."

"Perfectly, thank you. I have samples of a new line in leather gloves which have proved very popular with the people of the Westcountry. Let me show you the quality of these items and I'm sure that you will agree with me as to the reasonableness of their cost," replied Hardy.

Ching took the supple gloves in his hands and approved of the quality of their manufacture. He felt a severe headache grip his temples and, having secured an order for three gross of the gloves, rose from his chair to seek a drop of laudanum in his study. Thus he did not witness the gradual disappearance of Mr Hardy from his comfortable chair in the parlour.

Rose, the maidservant who ushered Hardy into the parlour, saw the whole thing. In the act of clearing the low table of the tea cups, she noticed that Mr Hardy had not touched his cup. As she straightened up with the charged tray in her hands, she glanced at Mr Hardy in his chair. His outline began to waver and dissolve. His form became thinner, his limbs almost skeletal. Gradually he faded from the chair, its brocade outline asserting itself through his transparent form. His face assumed the lines of a skull and then, he was gone. The chair remained as a mute testimony of his recent presence.

At Rose's hysterical scream Ching rushed back through the doorway. Jumping over the chaos of the dropped tray, he searched the room for any sign of Hardy. There was none, apart from the hat and stick in the front hall. Ching dashed out of the front door onto Broad Street, along the pavement to The White Hart and demanded to see Mr Pattison. He stood shocked before the landlord who listened to his emphatic words.

"Mr Hardy left strict and specific instructions that his room be not disturbed. Only in a dire emergency may I disregard those orders," said Pattison.

"I must find Mr Hardy. It is a matter of some urgency. He may have been taken ill and could have rushed back to his room for a remedy. We must open the door of his room and help him. It is no less than our duty, Mr Pattison," replied Ching.

"Very well Mr Ching. I am reluctant to open his room but we must help him if he is in distress. I will bring up the keys myself. I must insist that you accompany me, however, Mr Ching."

The two men climbed the stairs to room number four. The key grated in the lock as Mr Pattison carefully opened the door. Inside the room they found Hardy lying open-mouthed on the bed. His eyes were open and his face held an unmistakable expression of the utmost agony. He was quite dead and had obviously been so for some time. He lay in a pool of evil-smelling brown liquid which was beginning to solidify on the sheets and blankets of the bed. In the dead hands were the torn shreds of the clean white sheets put onto the bed only twenty-four hours ago.

"Out!" cried Pattison. "Tell no-one of this. Send for Dr Killock immediately and keep the door shut. We could have here a case of cholera!"

Half an hour later a shaken Dr Killock sat in Pattison's back parlour at the White Hart. He looked intently at the two men facing him.

"Mr Hardy has indeed succumbed to the dreaded cholera. He had been dead for at least twenty hours when I examined him. He died in agony during his first and last night under your roof. I am confident that if we take the necessary precautions, the disease will not spread. I myself took the utmost care when I examined him and, with God's grace have not contracted the disease," said Dr Killock.

That evening, under cover of dusk, Mr Geake the undertaker directed three men carrying a lead lined coffin into the back premises of the White Hart. Mr

Hardy's body was quietly removed and buried without the usual attentions to his person. He was buried in the soiled clothes in which he had died and, three weeks later, his body safely in the burial ground, a memorial service was held for him in the church of St Mary Magdalene. His family attending, the bells were rung in thanks for the containment of the deadly disease. As the joyful metallic peals broke in waves over Launceston, puzzled accountants in Worcester noted that Mr Hardy's last day of business in that town had been his best ever.

Tom Tucker

I will always remember Tom. Been an engineman man and boy, I have, and I've seen 'em come and go, what with nationalisation and the coming of the diesels. But Tom was different, a good fireman and, in his turn, a good driver. But different; more poetic than the usual run of the mill, though not stuck up, not in the least.

It were a few years after the ending of the Great War, around '23 or '24, it must have been, when I first clapped eyes on young Tom. Ashburton man he was, educated at the Grammar School before being taken on as a cleaner at Newton Abbot shed. Could easily have been taken on apprentice, but no, he wanted to become a driver. Set on it he was. He had a cheery smile and a good word for nearly everyone. Small chap he were, slight I think to call it. Tired easily but would not give up. Too young for the war but would have made a good soldier with that determination to let nothing beat him.

I remember when he passed as a driver. Young he was, but with all his determination, hard work and studying, he deserved it. His first booked turn was on the Ashburton branch, his home line of course. I was there to keep an eye on him, it being his first run out as driver.

We set out from Ashburton early in the morning, me firing for him, not only to keep my hand in but also to give him the opportunity to be in charge for the first time. He was in charge of one of Mr Churchward's small prairie tanks, a beautiful loco she was, built to run as sweetly backwards as forwards. With her slope tanks on either side of the boiler she was truly a beautiful sight. We had greased her up in swirls on the tanks and she was as clean as a new pin. With steam raised and the poppet valves lifted she was in charge of a longish train of empty cattle trucks and vans for the main line. With Tom's steady hand on the regulator we rattled and swayed out of the small yard at Ashburton. With hardly a puff of white smoke lifting from the chimney we drifted down the slight gradient towards the wide valley and Buckfastleigh. We left goods sheds, water cranes, warehouses and cottages behind as we dived beneath the short tunnel at the edge of the town to emerge in the fields on the long curve down to the River Dart. The angled slope of Brent Hill rose on the skyline as the white spire of Buckfastleigh church came into sight. With the empties bunched tight behind us we clattered over the Dart. Tom gently applied the brake and brought the train to a halt beneath the canopy of Buckfastleigh station where the token was exchanged and the down board pulled off.

The guard's whistle shrilled from the van and Tom opened up in fine style, just to show off really, as not much was required to start a train from Buckfastleigh. Smoke billowed as the Prairie dived under Paper Mill Bridge and, with rods clanking, we eased off down the straight to rumble over Nursery Pool Bridge, the track slightly skewed to one side from the narrowing of the broad gauge. With a shrill blast of the whistle we rounded Caddaford curve and plunged between orchards beside the Dart.

We came past the Stationmaster's house at Staverton a little on the fast side and Tom applied the brake to bring the train to rest at Staverton station, where a couple of open trucks were shunted in from behind the platform directly ahead of the Toad. Once again the gates were opened and the board pulled off.

The train gained speed on the curve between the joinery and the river. Tom whistled for the foot crossing and once again for the level crossing at Town Mill. It was here that things began to go wrong. As the train rounded the curve we could see that the gates were not yet fully open. A man was seen to be pushing hard on one of the gates. He was leaning with all his might on the far gate which appeared to be stuck in a half-open position. His grey head was bent over the top bar of the gate not far from the target. His good leg was stretched out along the rail to give him purchase while his other, wooden, leg jutted out at a useless angle. Tom shut off steam and jammed on the brakes in short order. Just before we hit, the gateman looked up with a hopeless dark grimace. Then, with a splintering crash, we slid squealing along the rails to smash both the gate and the struggling man to oblivion. I saw the man fall beneath the pony truck of the prairie, splinters of white-painted wood flying in all directions.

The train slid to a noisy halt surrounded by the wreckage of the gate. Then the whole scene was mercifully hidden by a great blast of steam as Tom blew out the drain cocks. After the shriek of steam only the tick of hot metal could be heard as the cloud drifted away.

Tom and I looked down to the tangled wreckage on the track. Most of the wood had been thrown clear of the crossing and the metal target lay in the leat. We jumped down from the loco expecting to find the shattered limbs and bloody twisted body of the crossing keeper under the buffer beam. But of him there was no sign. No blood stained the bright rails and no tattered cloth could be found entangled in the wheels or running gear.

Tom was shaking like a leaf and his face was a dirty grey.

"You know who that was, don't you?" he murmured. "We just hit old Uncle Joe Narramore. He lost his leg on the railway and kept the gate for years. The only trouble is that he died five years ago. I helped to carry his body from the keeper's cottage and loaded it up onto the train that waited on the crossing. A right cussing out I got from the driver for loading his coffin aboard the train head first instead of feet first. I never knew, of course, so I can't be to blame. But how could we hit a man who's been in his grave since the end of the war?" He looked desperately up at me. "Did we really see the same thing, Sam?"

"We certainly hit no live man, Tom," I replied.

We kicked and brushed the remains of the crossing gate from the buffer beam and set off as soon as we could. Fortunately we had not been required to protect the stopped train from any other traffic, having the tablet for sole possession of the line. But it was a relief to be off and to leave the scene of the accident behind us. As the train picked up speed once again, clattering over rail joints and swaying slightly, I could see that Tom was putting all his attention into driving. We eased round the long curve below Littlehempston Manor and picked up a fair turn of speed on the Royal Mile where Queen Victoria's royal trains used to be stabled for the night.

Under Hempstead Bridge with a cloud of downward deflected smoke and then a long wait for the main line at Ashburton Junction, the Totnes end of the branch. Tom wiped down all the handles and surfaces with an oily rag. Then he turned to me, his face pale in the light reflected from the firebox.

"Sam," he said. "Joe Narramore really was my uncle. He was my mother's oldest brother and always hated the Tuckers. Why this was so we never fathomed, but he would never speak to my father of any of his family. He was barely civil to me and, as he grew older, ceased speaking at all. Why he hated us I will never know; perhaps he grudged us our success. He seems to be reminding us that his hate will never go away."

"He's just a shade Tom, a spectre with no power to harm good Christian folk. I saw him too, but mark my words, boy, he'll do no harm to either of us. The destruction of the gate was not our fault, I will report a faulty catch at Totnes and we'll hear no more about it," I told Tom.

Eventually the ten o'clock express off Paddington passed along the main line in front of us, the board was pulled off and we rattled our empties over the bridge into Totnes Station. We shunted the opens onto the Quay branch and set the rest back into the yard. After negotiating the scissors crossing from the down platform to the up platform road we sat under the footbridge waiting for the off. An up express was signalled on the up through road so we were stuck once again.

It was a warm afternoon with sparks of light glinting up from the rails. We stood in the cab of the Prairie facing the curved 1 in 37 gradient under the road bridge in the direction of Plymouth. The loco hissed quietly and the clang of milk churns came occasionally from Dawe's Creamery behind the up platform. As the sliding window of the signal box slammed shut we knew that we were in for a lengthy wait.

A man walked slowly over the footbridge above our heads. We could hear the heel plates and hobnails of his boots on the decking and steps. Then Tom heard it.

"Sam," he said. "Hark to that! Do you hear it?"

I listened and could begin to hear the slow tread on the bridge decking of a one-legged man. The crash of a heavy boot was followed by the sharp tap of a wooden leg. Progress was steady though halting and the man walked slowly and painfully over our heads. I wondered how the man would sound as he climbed down the steep steps to the platform. I never knew; just as the dragging footsteps reached the top of the steps they suddenly ceased.

"It's him again, isn't it? He won't leave me alone. He can't stand my promotion to driver. Damn him to hell! He'll not have his way with me; I'll show him that he doesn't bother me!" Tom's face was pale and drawn but his determination showed through. He didn't bother to look up at the footbridge and waited quietly for the board to be pulled off to give us the road onto the branch.

The rest of the trip back to Ashburton light engine was uneventful. Before we left Totnes station we saw the new Castle Class engine "Carnaervon Castle" at the head of the Penzance to Paddington express, a sight we would never forget, all gleaming paint and polished brass. I could tell that Tom had his sights set high; one day he would drive the new Castles.

The summer wore on with Tom gaining in skill and confidence as a driver. Soon it would be time for him to be allocated to one of the mainline sheds to continue his rise up the links. Autumn came with the usual wet leaves on the track and sudden river fogs.

Towards the end of November Tom was asked to fire for me for a few early turns because Charlie Twigg was confined to bed with the 'flu. He was happy to do the early shift as fireman even though it meant getting up at half past three on freezing mornings, cycling down Chuley Road to the shed to light the fire in the Prairie and raise steam by half past six. He said that he always enjoyed prepping the loco and I took him at his word. Part of his duties was to wake me at half past six and I was very surprised when the church clock stuck seven and woke me up. I scrambled into my overalls and ran through the grey dawn down to the shed.

I could hear the hiss of steam and see the light of paraffin lamps in the high arched windows of the shed. What was Tom playing at, I wondered. Perhaps his watch had stopped; perhaps he had had an accident. Then I heard it, a sharp tapping sound from high up in the shed. Was it a branch from one of the overhanging trees? The day was still so I ruled that out.

I realised what I was hearing and ran round the end of the shed to see a hunched figure in corduroy trousers and an old GWR waistcoat walking unsteadily away from the shed in the direction of the churchyard. As he faded into the dimpsey I realised that one leg was rigid and tapped rhythmically on the ground as he walked. Despairingly I rushed into the shed to find that nearly everything was normal. The engine was in steam, cleaned and with the motion oiled. The shovel, prickers and fire irons were all in place and the rags and cotton waste all put away in their bins. The signing on book had been completed with the neat signature "T.D.Tucker" and the date and time correctly filled in. But on the line beneath was written in an untidy scrawl "J.Narramore" and the same date and time. Some of the letters had been scored deep into the paper, tearing it in places.

As realisation dawned upon me I heard a return of the rhythmic tapping that I had heard earlier. I looked up to see the polished toecap of a shoe tapping against the chimney of the loco in the rising breeze of dawn. I squinted against the yellow glare of the paraffin lamps to see Tom's limp body hanging from one of the shed's high beams. His neck was broken and his throat stretched; the grotesque shadow of the hanged man showed me that Tom had had one last visit from the malevolent spectre of his Uncle Joe Narramore.

Operation Paper Tiger

"Listen up gentlemen. Very few of you are going to get much sleep this weekend. It's not what you joined the Territorials for. We've organised a very interesting exercise for you with lots of fresh air and action.

D Squadron, Royal Devon Yeomanry, will form reconnaissance patrols and fighting patrols. The former will report intelligence back to the latter who will go in and destroy the enemy, or orange, forces. Patrols will now disperse to their briefings under the long hedgerow. Support troops will, in the meantime, assume an all-round defensive position."

Major Carew-Smyth turned on his heel and walked smartly over to the oak tree under which lay his table with the relevant maps. For once he felt well prepared for the exercise. Permission had been granted by all the farmers between Blackawton and Slapton Sands for the Army to use the rolling land with its deep coombs and high hedges for Operation Paper Tiger.

In the shade of the rough hedge Sergeant Black sat with his section squatting in front of him, weapons held pointing at the sky.

"Right, you cretins. We will form the forward reconnaissance patrol. Our task is to find out the strength and appearance of the enemy and to report it by radio or runner to Corporal Widdicombe's fighting patrol. Strict silence will be observed and you are only to engage the enemy if fired upon. The enemy could assume any disguise, even British army uniforms and kit. Be on your guard at all times and use the password when encountering any of our own forces. Lance Corporal Pearce and Private Smith, gun crew; Private Chope, radio; Privates Kearle, Wilson, Pope and Brown, riflemen; Lance Corporal Watkins, medic; Corporal Knight 2ic and myself section leader. Check your kit and be prepared to move out in ten minutes. Don't forget your camo cream or use cow shit if you've forgotten it. Check blank firing attachments and blanks in your ammo pouches. Private Pope, confirm for me the password for today, April 24th."

"Goat's scrotum, Sir."

"It's Sergeant! You dribbling halfwit. Are you a recruit or an embryo? Don't answer that, embryos can't talk. Wake up, Pope!"

"Sorry Sergeant. I will try to do better."

All along the hedgerow kneeling men wrapped black electrical tape round the arms and legs of their camouflaged combats to prevent the chafing noise that would give them away. They smeared evil smelling grease to their faces and poked grass and ferns into the sacking that wrapped their steel helmets. They moved stiffly, encumbered by their stiff webbing with ammunition pouches, small packs and water bottles. They carefully fed the crimped blank rounds into the magazines of their black self-loading rifles. Each man was sweating in the spring sunshine and slightly apprehensive of what the next two days and nights held for them. A solitary lark trilled high in the air above them, reminding the old sweats of Salisbury Plain.

At Black's murmured command they moved off, easing cramped muscles and stretching cautiously.

"Halt!" hissed Black. "Pope, I can hear the water sloshing in your bottle. Fill it up! Piss in it if you have to."

"Yes, Sergeant," replied Pope, quickly realising that he had a lot to learn if he were to survive his first weekend exercise.

The sweating patrol crept along the line of the hedge behind their sergeant. The riflemen tucked the pistol grips of their SLRs into the gaps between their webbing belts and their smocks.

The radio operator cursed the dead weight of his instrument and the gunner and his number two distributed various bits of kit around their webbing. Black and Corporal Knight stopped frequently to consult the map and observe any movement in the fields and hillsides that lay all around them.

It was a warm and tedious day with the temptation to drowse at every stop. It was hard to maintain a decent level of concentration when everyone knew that it was just one more weekend exercise. The men tripped over their heavy boots and cursed when puttees came loose in the brambles. Pope found himself thinking about the last war, now nearly fifty years in the past. Hadn't the whole of this area been evacuated for some reason?

It was obvious to Sergeant Black that the enemy would come from the seaward side of the area. The patrol was heading laboriously towards the coast. Trees were becoming scarcer and more bent by the force of the salt winds. The quality of the light was changing with the proximity of the sea over the next ridge. He could not yet hear the sound of the waves breaking on the shingle but felt the presence of the flat ocean.

Black waved the patrol flat with a sweep of his hand. Every man went quietly down beside another interminable hedgerow, eyes on the man in front. The sergeant had heard faint voices from a field ahead. He wormed his way to a gateway where he had an unobstructed view of a grass field that sloped away to the shore. At the bottom were some low green tents and a jeep.

"The orange forces have disguised themselves as Yanks, Corps." he whispered to Corporal Knight. "We can't tell how many of them there are from here. We must stage a diversion to draw them out and count their numbers."

He signalled with his pumped closed fist for the gun team who crept up quietly. He motioned to them to take a position in a hole in the hedge twenty yards to the left where their arc of fire would cover the whole enemy camp. He positioned the riflemen along the hedge at twenty yard intervals and placed the radio in the middle. Then he put Knight between the patrol and himself and set off fifty yards to the left along the hedge.

The diversion was simple. While planning it he realised how few men he had to work with. Good men certainly, but not as experienced as those he had commanded in Northern Ireland. From his position in the hedge he threw a smoke grenade high into the air so that it fell near to the camp. It exploded with a muffled crack sending orange smoke drifting away from the tents and the jeep. The lounging sentry jumped and looked all round him unaware of Black's concealed position. A whistle blew and men in pot helmets swarmed out of the tents, carbines in their hands. A few held Thompson sub-machine guns and ran in a crouching posture in Black's direction. He signalled silently to Knight to warn the patrol to keep their heads down.

The Americans ran towards the hedge. Black was impressed by their appearance; he could see their dusty brown boots and stained gaiters. Their combats were a dull olive green, dirty and worn. Several men wore black chevrons on their arms with curved rockers beneath. He could hear their boots thudding on the dry turf and the occasional clank of equipment. Not a word was spoken as they approached. Black wondered if they were re-enactors, perhaps from Plymouth. If only he could hear them speak. Then he would know.

So far the recce patrol had not been spotted. Black signalled the number "sixty" to Knight who signalled back "seventy". The Americans reached the hedge and sheltered behind it; now only ten feet of stone, earth and vegetation separated them from Black. The rest of the patrol lay round a curve in the bank so only Black was at risk of detection. He thought he had got away with it when a shot rang out from the hedge fifty yard to his right.

"Damn!" thought Black. "Private Bloody Pope! I'll have him in the guardhouse for negligent discharge before his feet can touch the ground."

As the Americans crouched at the foot of the bank Knight signalled the gun team through the gate to enfilade the Americans before they could respond. They were a split second too late. As they opened up with a short burst, a Private First Class fired at them across the curving line of the hedge, hitting them both with deadly accuracy. Pearce was shot through the head and went down with a spastic flailing of arms. Smith fell sideways clutching his stomach and lay writhing in the gateway, rounds spilling from his open pouches.

"No! Stop!" Black shouted at the top of his voice. He couldn't believe that the orange forces were using live rounds on this exercise. "Medic, to the gun team. Hurry! Radio for a helicopter now!" he yelled.

The Americans were strangely quiet. There was no talking nor sudden movements. There was no noise at all except the sound of the lark and the early drone of bees. The Americans seemed to be dissolving, to be melting away. Even the outlines of their tents and jeep wavered and faded before the patrol's astonished gaze.

One man noticed nothing of this. Lance Corporal Watkins ran, his medical kit banging at his side, towards the two still figures in the gateway. Blood pooled from Pearce's shattered head, one eye hung down his bloody cheek. Smith appeared to still be alive. He groaned as he lay twisted over the barrel of the LMG. Watkins reached the man, his mind strangely clear. As he did so Pearce sat up, rubbed his eyes, swore, and took a long drink from his water bottle. Smith rolled over, the brass rounds tinkling as they fell from him. He sat up blinking. Watkins dropped his wound dressings and morphine needle and stood frozen to the spot looking down at the two men. There was not a mark on either man. Watkins did not know whether he was more shocked at the appearance of shattered bodies or untouched men. He sank down onto the grass, his eyes staring.

On the other side of the hedge the Americans' field was now completely empty. No trace was left of the Company of U.S. Infantry who had crouched only a few feet away, the sour smell of sweat and stale tobacco tainting the air around them.

"Well I'm buggered..." said Sergeant Black quietly, quite at a loss for words for once. Then sense returned. "Private Chope, have you raised anyone on the radio?"

"No Sergeant," Chope replied. "The damned battery's completely drained. I can't get any signal at all."

"Just as well you didn't call for a helicopter. Knight, what do you make of this?" As Knight scratched his chin the gun crew rose shakily to their feet and checked their kit. They threw the

61

empty cartridge cases into the hedge and sat against the hedge to clean the gun. The rest of the patrol crouched silently, their rifles in their hands.

"What did we all see just now?" asked a puzzled Watkins. "Were those men hit or not? Is this some kind of clever trick?"

All the men present agreed that they had seen and heard the same things. Pope's negligent discharge temporarily forgotten, the patrol set warily off to reach the coast. As they crossed an open field in single file, the roar of a naval bombardment smote their ears and a gout of black smoke rose into the sky from just ahead of them. Quietly they took up defensive positions behind another hedgerow. The rattle of small arms fire and the deeper boom of artillery came to them from the area of the beach. Hoarse shouts and screams reached their ears over the revving of engines and the clatter of tank tracks.

Black slowly raised his head above the tangle of the bank. Spread below him was a scene of carnage and utter disorder. Tiny men ran up the shingle beach, their weapons winking light as they fired. From time to time a man fell and rolled onto the sand. Tanks churned up the beach, slewing as they reached the long ribbon of coast road. Bright flashes hurt his eyes as shells landed in a seemingly random pattern, sometimes among the troops. Long tangles of barbed wire lay untidily along whole stretches of beach and, in the midst of the surging disorder black oily smoke rose from the ruins of the hotel just behind the beach.

Lines of blunt ended landing craft approached the surf line from larger ships out in Start Bay. The light twinkled from the gentle swell which bore the packed landing craft towards the chaos of the crowded beach. Black brought the binoculars to his eyes. In the breaking waves and further out in the bay he could make out dark figures floating limply in lifejackets. Many seemed to be floating upside down, their boots protruding from the water in place of their heads.

Numbed by the horror of the scene below him Black realised that the whole landing was now happening in utter silence. He saw the bright flash of exploding ordinance but heard no percussion. The men on the beach were shouting silent orders and the tanks continued to roll and churn in complete silence.

Black took his eyes off the beach and the sparkling waters of the bay. He looked up at the small lark trilling in the empty air above his head. He looked back at the sweep of the now deserted bay. A few people in civilian clothes walked on the shingle; occasionally one would bend down to pick up a found object. Long lines of seaweed and the occasional bleached tree trunk lay along the high tide mark. The shingle lay undisturbed in a three mile curve from Torcross to Strete Gate and beyond. The burning hotel with its blackened beams and jagged masonry was now just a car park with a few cars dotted along the seaward edge and the granite memorial with its flagpoles adjacent.

Black slid helplessly down the bank. He gathered the patrol around him.

"The radio is out of action. We have no means of communication except word of mouth. We must make a report as soon as possible and stick together at all times. Normally I would send a runner but feel that with all this weird shit happening we are all vulnerable. Look sharp; we'll work our way back to Forces Cross and report our intelligence to HQ," he said.

Night was beginning to fall as the men set out up the hill away from the silent beach. No-one attempted even to whisper; each man was alone with his thoughts trying to make some sort of sense of what he had seen. The westering sun cast ruddy shadows onto tense faces beneath the rims of steel helmets. The soldiers moved quietly, glancing about them as they moved inland. Black, at the point of the patrol was convinced that some sort of trick had been played on them and his fear was tinged with a dark fury.

The moon rose behind them as they checked their position and trudged uphill towards distant Forces Cross, a crossroads on the main Totnes to Dartmouth road which contained in its fork a small and isolated pub. The tired men knew instinctively that the exercise was nearly over; tomorrow at the hastily arranged debriefing the illusion, the psychological warfare or whatever it was would be explained and rounds of drinks would be enjoyed by all the weary warriors. At least they would get a good night's sleep rather than tramping around the countryside chasing phantoms.

After hours of consulting maps and compasses, straining eyes to detect enemy patrols and staggering over ploughed fields, the patrol approached Forces Cross at two o'clock in the morning. The men crouched in a shadowy clump of trees staring at several arc lights that lit up a field hidden behind a high bank. They could hear the revving of powerful earthmoving equipment and the low murmur of voices.

Black crept to the bottom of the bank and hauled himself into the cover of the high hedge. He could make out the dim lights of the pub to the right of the arc lights on their poles. He faintly heard words spoken with American accents between the bursts of sound from the bulldozers digging deep trenches in the field.

"Hey, Van Nostrand, there's nobody with the dead guys!"

"They're going nowhere, dude. Poor bastards never stood a chance. They was mown down like corn and now they're stacked up like cordwood ready to go into the ground. Makes you sick, don't it."

"Yeah, sure does. Break out the luckies will you Bud."

Black had heard enough. He slid down the bank and rejoined the crouching men. He instructed them to quietly make their way to a shadowed corner of the field where several dark tarpaulins covered shapes that were vaguely and sickeningly familiar.

Black and Knight bent to peel back the heavy cover. Under it lay rows of sprawling men, their bone-white faces bleached further by the moon. Filthy hands lay at angles on the grass beside the shadowed bulk of twisted bodies. Here and there an arm stuck straight up from a shoulder and booted feet cast their random shadows on the short grass.

"No!" shouted Pope. "Make it stop. It's too much. I can't bloody stand it!" The arc lights dimmed, the voices and revving machinery stopped, the dead men at their feet melted into the ground.

An unmistakably British voice called irritably out: "Password!"

"Goat balls!" yelled Black. A shot rang out as Black shouted "scrotum!" at the top of his voice.

"Right lads, listen up. The damned exercise is cancelled! We've been trying to reach you all day on the radio. Someone at County Hall decided that this weekend, being the fiftieth anniversary of the main events of Operation Tiger, the American Forces' practice landings, would be the wrong one for our little exercise. The brigadier had to agree so that put the kybosh on our fun and games. I'm sorry you have had a stroll in the country for nothing. Meet me in the pub when you've cleaned yourselves up," called Major Carew-Smyth.

"Did you send anyone out after us, Sir?" asked Black.

"Good God, no, Sergeant. Who do you think we are, the bloody U.S. cavalry?"

<u>Veyther</u>

The Warren House Inn crouched on the side of a moorland hill, miles from any other habitation. It lay near to the centre of Dartmoor fully exposed to the south-westerly wind. To the north the trackless waste rose to the vast Fernworthy Forest and the precipitous high moor. The eroded seams of ancient tin workings stretched to the south where more tors reared against the sky. The narrow undulating ribbon of the Moretonhampstead to Tavistock road stretched east and west for miles across the dun uplands before descending to the lush green Devon farmlands.

It was to this isolated hostelry that the venerable Bill Miners, retired grazier and haulier of livestock, came to sit before the fire and talk to locals and visitors alike on most evenings of the year. He would trudge the weary and windy two miles from his tiny cottage in the valley at Postbridge and home again at closing time.

One Friday evening in early March Bill was sitting with his pint of scrumpy in his usual settle beside the glowing logs in the granite fireplace in the snug of the inn. Inside all was warmth and relaxation, while outside the flimsy door the chill east wind hooted and spat raindrops in the dusk onto the panes of the small windows. The occasional land rover passed on the road while the only sound to be heard apart from the fitful gusts of the wind was the thump of the generator beside the rambling building.

At last the door opened to admit a walker as well as a boisterous packet of wind. The man carefully closed the door before removing his cagoule, gaiters, map case and waterproof hat. He ordered a pint of Tamar and came over to warm himself at the fire.

"Come var, 'ev ee?" asked Bill, wiping his nose on the sleeve of his malodorous tweed jacket.

"I've walked along Hamel Down from Widecombe," replied the stranger. "Got a bit lost in the old tin workings just south of here. If I hadn't seen the lights of the inn I would still be in there wandering around."

"Tis not a good place to be walking in after dark," said Bill. "Many year ago my old veyther veil down one of they addits in the dark. If he hadn't landed on the swelled out carcase of a pony he'd a been dead as a rag. He managed to clamber out in good time."

"In that case I count myself lucky to have arrived," said the walker. "I will sleep like a log here after supper and a couple more pints. My name's Charles Crane and I'm heading west towards Tavistock tomorrow." He produced a crumpled Odnance Survey map and a well used Crossing's Guide.

"Bill Miners, of Postbridge; Dartmoor born and bred. Nothing would persuade me to sleep in this inn of a night. I'd sooner walk the two miles back to Postbridge in all weathers than stop 'ere."

"Why would you not sleep here? It's comfortable enough and the food is good, from what I can smell of it," asked Crane.

"If I told 'ee you would certainly think twice about it. I better not, I ain't about to give the place a bad name. 'Tis better you didn't know. No tales no pack drill," intimated Bill. Crane liked a good yarn and offered Bill another pint of Old Screwface.

"I don't mind if I do. 'Twill ease my long walk home to my cottage."

After a while Crane glanced round the rough beams and panelled walls of the pub. A fire burned in a granite fireplace at each end of the bar. Faded photographs of the hard winter of '63 adorned the bar. Spats of hard rain blew with increasing fury against the windows.

Bill spoke at last: "In the summer of '29, when I were a boy, the landlord here upped and shot 'imself dead behind the bar just before closing time. 'Twas said that he was a haunted man and that he could take no more of it. This place 'as been cursed for nigh on a hundred years."

"Please carry on, I love ghost stories," said Crane, leaning forward to catch the old man's words.

"Over a 'undred years ago a traveller, like yourself, put up at this inn. Landlord showed'n to his room and left 'n with some candles. The traveller looked around 'is room and found all the usual things: bed, washstand with jug and ewer. Under the window 'ee found a sort of built-in chest with a hinged lid. Course 'ee lifted the lid to see what wus inside of 'un. Imagine 'is surprise when 'ee saw, in the light of the candle, a dead man lying in the chest. 'Is big toes was tied together wi' binder cord and 'is arms was laid across 'is chest. 'Twas plain er 'ad been dead fur some considerable time. The traveller rushed downstairs to rouse the landlord.

"Don't 'ee worry, m' dear," said landlord. "'Tis nothing to get worked up about, 'tis only feyther; us ev salted 'n down against the spring when us can take'n to Lydford in order to bury 'n proper. Zoil be too frozen just now to dig 'n a grave so us 'as to wait patiently vur the turn o' the season."

The traveller went up to bed but 'er didn't sleep too sound. He left the inn whisht and pale next day and walked away over the moor. But Veyther didn't rest easy either, 'er 'ad been disturbed and was like to ramble about. Landlord 'ad 'n buried come the

71

spring but 'er couldn't get rid of 'n. I bid you Good Evening and Good Night. I'm off down the road to my snug little cottage beside the East Dart and I hope you rest well in your room."

Bill stood up, stretched, and walked unsteadily over to the door, pulling on his coat as he went. He went out into the howling darkness and walked steadily downhill home along the shoulder of the road with only the occasional passing car and sleepy sheep for company.

Crane looked once more round the snug and decided that it was time for him to turn in. With luck he would be asleep before Bill reached the front door of his cottage by the Dart at Postbridge. He climbed the steep stairs and walked along the narrow passage. His room lay at the far end with its window facing south over the deserted road and the abandoned tin workings. It was a small room, quite snug, although buffeted by the occasional blast of wind. The bed was comfortable and, in place of a jug and ewer, a small washbasin provided accessible hygiene.

Crane lay gratefully down on the soft bed feeling clean and relaxed. He felt sure that no ghost would bother him tonight. If he woke to an apparition he would throw his dirty socks at it and turn his face to the wall. He slept exceptionally well, no dreams disturbed his slumber, and awoke refreshed with sunlight streaming in at his small window.

As he pulled on clean socks over slightly tender feet Crane looked over at the window. It came as no surprise that, under the small paned sash, there was a long window seat with a hinged lid. Crane examined it and decided that it was as old as the room and therefore of considerable antiquity. The planks were of oak and the iron hinges hand forged. He could not resist opening the heavy lid. It creaked open to reveal, not a shrivelled corpse in the attitude of one long dead, but a musty emptiness with the sour smell of air not often disturbed. With a slight shudder Crane closed the lid, collected his things and thumped down the staircase to the excellent breakfast that awaited him in the snug.

The new day had dawned clear and clean with all traces of rain past and wisps of high cloud trailing the high tors. Crane enjoyed his breakfast and paid his bill to the man behind the bar. He carefully tied his bootlaces and consulted the map, deciding to walk due north of the inn onto the high moor before turning west at the Grey Wethers, concentric stone circles that lay near the edge of Fernworthy Forest.

Crane stood on the road in front of the inn and breathed the clean moorland air. Shouldering his pack, he trudged round the side of the building where the generator thumped forlornly away. He lengthened his stride on the rising springy turf as he felt a slight breeze on his right cheek. "All well and good so far," he thought. He would cross the upper valley of the East Dart, have a look at the primitive tangle of Wistman's Wood and be in the vicinity of Two Bridges in time for a late lunch. He certainly would not reach Tavistock tonight, even with fair weather, so would find a place for the night at Princetown.

He strolled easily over the rough ground. In places it was waterlogged and clumps of coarse reeds and bog cotton warned him where lay featherbeds or areas of bog where the water never drained into the impervious granite below. Crane easily recognised these dangerous areas and detoured around them. He found the old peat cuttings tedious to walk through, having constantly to step up and down as the levels changed. It was important to keep his eyes raised to the horizon in order to keep walking in a straight line. From time to time Crane stopped to check his compass bearing, noting occasional swings of the needle because of the old tin workings. He was enjoying the walk and the immediacy of the small problems he had to overcome to find his way over the ridges and valleys.

Back in the Warren House Inn Crane's bed lay unmade and his room as yet unprepared for its next occupant. There was a slight creak from the long box below the window and, slowly, the heavy lid began to hinge upwards. There was a crash as it fell open but nobody saw the tall, thin figure that slowly climbed out to stand before the window, all detail obliterated by the bright sun blazing through the small panes. With unknown purpose the figure walked lightly across the wooden planks of the floor, its long toenails scratching on the worn wood. It was seeking something or someone and was glad to be out of its long confinement. It followed the long upstairs corridor that was so familiar to it and came down the stairs, across the empty snug and out of the open door into the bright light of morning. It knew which direction to take and wasted no time in setting off towards the Grey Wethers.

Crane stood in the middle of one of the circles marvelling at the symmetry of the long granite slabs set so perfectly in relation to their fellows. He looked away to the succession of dips and ridges to the west which would lead him to the East Dart and to Wistman's Wood. Glancing to his left, he saw a tall man walking towards him on a ridge top less than a mile away. He seemed to move lightly and rapidly, hardly seeming to touch the ground.

Crane set off, not feeling inclined to be sociable at that time in the morning. He was slightly unnerved to see that the man was changing direction as if to close the distance between them. Yet the man made no sign of welcome, nor did he try to attract Crane's attention. Crane pretended to ignore the man. With a feeling of slight irritation he trudged on towards a distant tor that rose into the blue sky ahead of him. Once over the ridge he could change direction slightly and lose the other man easily.

A couple of hours later Crane saw the isolated tangle of Wistman's Wood in the valley below him. The ancient twisted oaks were all that remained of the dense woods that covered the moor in the dark ages before the changing climate had denuded the uplands. It was an eerie place, a good two miles up the valley from the nearest house, perched on the valley's side with only the raven's croak and the distant noise of water to relieve the feeling of solitude. Crane was relieved to have arrived. He sat down on a mossy rock just under the twisted canopy of oak and took off his boots. A sound of snapping twigs below him forced him to the realisation that he was not alone. From behind a huge rock at the bottom of the wood came the thin man who had been following Crane. Long grey hair straggled from the bony head. Arms that looked more like sticks hung from shoulders from which all trace of fat had long gone. The shape of the rib cage protruded from the ragged strips of shirt which had once covered the still chest. Only the eyes seemed alive; they glared redly and balefully at Crane as he sat powerless on his rock.

"Hello there, what do you want? Who are you?" Crane felt his voice rise in panic as the creature came over and around the rocks and roots straight towards him, red eyes fixed on his. He heard no answer to his question but the word "Veyther" rose rustily in his mind as he blacked out.

Crane was not missed for a couple of days. Finally his mates at the Cartographical office in Taunton suspected that all was not well and contacted the police at Moretonhampstead. The Dartmoor Rescue Volunteers were sent out and, after half a day's searching of the northern part of the moor, finally found a body in a stream between Wistman's Wood and Two Bridges. The features were unrecognisable but the dead man was finally identified as Crane by his sister from Yorkshire. How he came to be submerged in the stream was a complete mystery.

The police found that he had been dragged for over a mile from the top of Wistman's Wood. He seemed to have offered little resistance to his killer, the only trace of whom was a long broken fingernail clutched in Crane's fingers. His throat had been torn open and his face and scalp ripped off by his assailant who offered not even the ghost of a motive for the violent killing.

Babbacombe Lee

On a lowering day in late winter Gerald walked from his office in Southernhay up the hill to Northernhay Park to look across the misty valley at Exeter Prison. He stood beside the empty bandstand looking over the dim roofs of Central Station at the long brick building with its numerous barred windows; sightless eyes looking down at a means of escape so near yet so far away. The prison seemed peaceful, yet Gerald knew of the desperation and the overcrowding behind the placid walls.

He stood with the curved lawns at his back, a solitary figure muffled in an expensive coat, a world away from the unhappy men confined behind brick walls a few hundred yards across the valley. In a few minutes' time he would enter the doors of the prison for the first time.

He was no white collar criminal, just a structural engineer who was to make a report on the suitability of the conversion of a disused shed into office accommodation. Space was at a premium in the prison and the Home Office was keen to increase the number of inmates by using areas that had previously been neglected or forgotten.

Gerald turned into the cutting east wind and walked past the lofty war memorial with its soldiers and sailors perched over the neat lawns. Under the crumbling red stones of the castle walls a drunk slept in a red sleeping bag, empty cans of cider lying at angles round his head. Gerald walked briskly down the sloping path to the park lodge and iron gates that led to Queen Street. He turned right past the suburban crescent of shops that announced Central Station, crossed the almost unseen railway bridge and turned right into New North Road at the statue of Sir Redvers Buller. Soon he came to the imposing doors of the prison. He rang the bell and waited in the chill. The growl of a train reached him from the tracks below and he heard a dog bark from the park behind the trees.

The heavy door was opened and Gerald was ushered in to a pleasant office painted an institutional cream. He was given a badge marked *Gerald Seymour Berry; Brown, Endicott and Berry, Structural Engineers* and was hurried through narrow corridors to a remote corner of the prison where two outer walls met under an enclosed lean-to roof. The vast room was musty with disuse and damp and cluttered with old lengths of timber and broken tubular chairs.

"If it's alright with you, I'll leave you here until four thirty," said the man in warder's uniform. "I'm afraid I'll have to lock you in for your own safety. Rules is rules and you wouldn't want to meet some of the men who are confined in here at the moment. I'll see you later, Sir." The door slammed and the key grated in the lock. Gerald was amused to think that he too was a prisoner. He had his mobile phone and could phone the office if he needed anything. Without it he could shout and scream all day and nobody would come and see if he were alright.

He set about measuring the enclosed space and moving some of the lumber that cluttered the floor. Under it he found some rather fine granite setts from the nineteenth century. The whole structure seemed sound and appeared to date, like the floor, from the early years of Queen Victoria's reign. Gerald found himself wondering what the shed had been used for and why it was no longer used for anything except untidy storage.

After a couple of hours' hard work and many calculations he sat down on a roll of dusty canvas. It was cold in the unheated shed and Gerald felt overcome by drowsiness. He thought that if he could close his eyes for a minute his head would clear and he could resume his calculations. His head nodded as he dozed for a minute.

He came sharply awake at the sound of the shed doors grating open. Men in blue uniforms were dragging a heavy timber structure in from outside. It had begun to rain and water dripped from the beams of the heavy scaffold as it was edged over the threshold. Gerald wondered why a gallows was being brought into the shed at this stage. The sweating men muttered instructions at each other and appeared totally unaware of Gerald's presence in the shed. One of the warders glanced over at Gerald and seemed to look straight through him. Gradually the scaffold was manoeuvred into place. It stood a good twenty feet high and sat squarely in the middle of the lofty shed. The warders passed round a brown earthenware flagon of cider. "Surely," thought Gerald. "These men are not allowed to drink on duty."

The chief warder produced a hemp rope which he formed into a noose by pulling the free end through a metal eyelet. He reached up to pass the rope through an iron hook on the highest beam of the scaffold. Jokingly he waved the noose at the fat man with the cider jar. Gerald heard his words as if from a far distance.

"Put this'un round your bleddy neck ye worthless bastard, Pascoe!" he shouted.

"You'll have need of'n avore I do," replied the offended man.

Two warders carried a heavy sack of sand up the wooden steps of the scaffold. The shed door opened once again and in came a small neat man dressed in a dark suit and a white shirt with a round collar. He took off his bowler hat and placed it carefully on a wooden chair near the door. The blue uniformed warders became respectful and serious.

"Good morning Mr Berry," said the chief warder. "I trust you had a good journey to Exeter last night, Sir."

"Yes thank you, Mr Courtenay," replied Berry. "Make ready the trap. The scaffold has been sitting out in the wet for too long and I would like to check that the trapdoors will open properly."

The two men attached the bag of sand to the noose and stood smartly to the side of the high platform. Mr Berry climbed the steps until he too stood beneath the shed's lofty roof. He took a couple of brisk steps to the lever at the platform's edge and pulled it smoothly. Gerald started as the two trap doors opened with a crash that echoed round the silent shed. The sack hung slowly revolving at the end if the rope, its squat bulk now stretched into an elongated shape. Some wet sand dribbled through small holes in the hessian to fall onto the damp granite floor.

Gerald saw the whole scene through a damp fog which seemed to swirl between the high black scaffold and himself. He saw Berry climb carefully down the steep steps and leave the shed. He heard the warders discuss how the hangman would calculate the drop in order to cleanly break the neck of the condemned man without decapitating him. He wondered who the condemned man was before realising with a start that no-one had been hanged in an English prison since 1965. Had he been dreaming? Had his over-active imagination got the better of him once more?

With a start he realised that he was cold and damp and he heard heavy footsteps approaching the door. With a crash it swung open to admit weak winter sunlight and a warder in a very much more modern uniform than those he had seen a few minutes ago.

"Are you ready to leave, Mr Berry," asked the warder in a sympathetic voice. "I can't wait to see this gloomy old building converted into nice modern offices. It used to be the execution shed until forty years ago and I don't like to be in here on my own for any length of time. Call me silly if you like but I'm sure that the fabric of the building contains traces of the emotions of the men who worked and died in here."

"I'm sure you're right Mr Mortimore," Gerald replied. "I suppose that in my case only time will tell."

The two men walked out into the smoky winter dusk to see the red sun sinking behind the Haldon Hills streaking the low clouds with crimson shafts.

Next morning Gerald was back at work in the execution shed. He was pleased with his calculations and felt no sense of oppression or foreboding caused by his surroundings. He determined not to nap on the job again and looked forward to the favourable reception of his planning and calculations. But by mid morning he was tired again and ready for a short rest on the roll of dusty canvas. No sooner had he sat down than he was aware of movement in the shed. The black scaffold was back with four men standing solemnly on it, one of whom was an enormously fat chaplain in canonical robes. Two men brought in a pinioned prisoner, a tall gaunt man with dark deep set eyes and a powerful jaw. Gerald recognised Berry the hangman and Courtenay the chief warder. Both men helped the prisoner up the steep stairs to the gallery. From the platform the prisoner looked around at the airy spaces of the shed before turning back to the four solemn men who surrounded him. Gerald caught the flash of a quick wink from the prisoner to the chaplain who surreptitiously winked back.

Berry stepped forward and buckled a strap around the man's ankles. He placed a white hood over the man's head, the noose loosely round his neck and positioned him on the heavy twin trap doors. The chaplain moved his bulk closer to the trap and opened his prayer book.

The Prison Governor spoke in a husky voice: "John Edward Lee, you have been found guilty of murder and sentenced to hang by the neck until dead. This sentence is about to be carried out according to due process of law. May God have mercy on your soul. Do you have any last words to say before..."

Lee's rough Devon brogue filled the shed. "Sir, I go to my death an innocent man. I never killed Miss Keyse at Babbacombe nor did I steal from her. May God forgive you for what you are about to do."

The chaplain murmured a few prayers of which Gerald could catch only the gist. He heard the soft "amens" of the assembled company before a momentary silence filled the space.

Berry pulled back the lever in a smooth fluid motion. Lee's body jerked spasmodically but he remained standing on the trap. Gerald tensed himself for the jarring crash of the oak doors and held his breath when nothing happened. The chaplain moved away from the trap and Lee, still hooded, was led away down the steps to a side room while the trap was oiled and tested once more with a heavy bag of sand. Once more the doors crashed open. Gerald reflected that Lee must have heard the echoes from his side room.

Soon he was led back and the whole process was repeated. Prayers were said and the lever was pulled in the sinuous motion peculiar to Berry. Once more nothing happened. In a loud voice the Governor ordered a shaking Lee to be taken immediately back to his cell and given breakfast. Damp fog swirled round the gallows and Gerald decided that he could stay no longer in the vast damp confines of the shed.

He called the office on his mobile and the concerned warder escorted him back to the cream painted office and gave him a cup of tea.

"Are you quite sure that you are alright Sir?" enquired Mortimore. "That place gives me the creeps. Have you finished in there for today?"

"I will come back tomorrow to complete the survey and check some of the calculations. Please would you be so kind as to see me out Mr Mortimore."

Gerald stepped out into the street with a great sense of relief. Behind him reared the ugly brick prison with its barred windows and grim secrets; before him lay the city with its trees, spires and the human interaction from which he seemed to have been separated for so long. He would walk to the Library and take some time to research the events he had witnessed in such a mysterious fashion. He would satisfy himself of the truth or otherwise of the botched execution he had apparently just seen.

Once in the quietness of the Library he logged on and typed "John Edward Lee" into the search engine. Gerald was amazed to see the gaunt features of the man he had seen pinioned and hooded on the gallows. The receding hair, protruding cheekbones and massive jaw were familiar to him in an uncanny way. He learned that, on 23rd February 1885, the events he had seen took place in the exact order of his memory.

Next he typed in the words "Berry, Executioner" and saw an image of the small neat man who he found turned out to be his great uncle. He saw a distinct family resemblance in the tidy features and well proportioned limbs.

He now knew what had happened but was determined to find out why. Perhaps the crafty wink between Lee and the chaplain had something to do with why the trap had failed twice to open.

Next day it was with a distinct sense of apprehension that Gerald found himself once more in the dusky vastness of the shed. Once again the vision of the execution returned to him. This time the prisoner was obviously sedated and had to be half carried up the steps to the gallery. Once more Lee was strapped and hooded, the rope was placed around his neck with the eyelet beneath the left ear. Once again the prayers were read and the chaplain moved sideways towards the trap doors.

With a thrill of recognition Gerald saw how the chaplain's bulk warped one of the decking planks against the side of one of the closed trap doors, wedging it closed. When Berry pulled the lever, the bolt slid easily back but both doors remained jammed firmly closed. Gerald was powerless to change the events before his eyes. He was as impotent as a ghost. All he had was his surveyor's knowledge of a chain of events that had happened over a hundred years earlier.

That evening he returned to his thatched cottage in Abbotskerswell reflecting wryly that John "Babbacombe" Lee had also lived in the village. Indeed Lee had returned to it after his eventual release from prison more than twenty years after the failed execution and had lived there for some time before moving away to the Tavistock area. Gerald sat in his cosy living room in front of a roaring fire. He had had an interesting day but had a lot to think about and sort out in his mind. More research was needed than that he had undertaken in the library. He had plenty of time to think; his wife was away on a Union course in Birmingham and would not be home until the weekend.

As he sat drowsily in his comfortable chair he heard the sharp sound of pebbles flung against his front door. Irritably he rose from his chair and walked out into the hall to see who had played this trick on him. He heard a crash as the front gate was kicked open. Angrily he opened the front door. His blood turned to ice as he saw a tall man in a rough woollen suit trudging up the path towards him. Too late he recognised the sunken eyes, the lantern jaw and the axe gripped in the large bony hand. `

Floreat Totnesia

There were five of us, all Sixth Form students from King Edward VI School, Totnes, in the late 1960s, the time of the Viet Nam conflict and the Cold War. We had all been at the Grammar School, had all done reasonably well at our O levels and had all passed into the Sixth Form. We were all studying A level History and were all reasonably interested in mediaeval history.

There was Henry, a farmer's son and a keen rugby player. He was a plain speaker and had taken his punishment on the rugby field. He was honest, and his broken nose showed that he didn't mind taking his lumps. His knowledge of mediaeval history was deeper than ours but he never flaunted it at our expense.

Then there was Nick, destined as officer material for the Formed Arses of the Crown. He had leadership potential and asserted it at every opportunity. But he had a good brain and most of us respected him in a grudging sort of way. He was the guy we all would like to have been if we had had the moral fibre. We were all slightly in awe of him although we realised that we would one day outgrow what he had become.

There was Charles, the brightest of us all. He would give up a promising career as a doctor to become a vicar in the north of England. Like Henry, he was a Devonian with a great honesty which extended to plain speaking when the rest of us were trying to impress girls or our mates. He had a brilliant mind and an integrity which the rest of us sometimes lacked.

John was quiet and always thoughtful. After the Sixth Form he went to university in Wales and read geology. He worked for a while in the goldfields of South Africa, came home after the premature death of his father and became a furniture restorer after a further course of study. He returned to his beloved home town of Totnes and his wise and bearded presence has been a town fixture ever since.

Then there is me. I surprised myself by going to university in the north of England. I never ended up in the Army, except as a Territorial. Like Henry, I became a teacher and came back to Totnes. After teaching French for many years I left King Edward VI College and became a writer with moderate success. It is left to me to chronicle what happened to the five of us, so disparate but so similar in our aspirations to transcend our origins while returning eventually to our roots. I am unique in that out of the five I am the only one left alive.

On an early Autumn Saturday in 1967 we had decided to walk to Berry Pomeroy Castle to make notes on the transition from mediaeval defensive to later domestic architecture. We decided to walk from Totnes and, equipped with parkas, combat jackets and chukka boots, we set off on a brilliant sunny day from Totnes. Nick had the map and had worked out a route using green lanes and woodland paths. We went along for a laugh, but also because we valued the chance to walk through beautiful countryside and explore a beautiful castle in the middle of a forest.

We left Totnes behind and walked out on the mediaeval ridgeway on a glorious day. The sun shone in a clear blue sky with only a few fluffy clouds drifting above us. We turned up a stony track towards the dark woods and left the swoop of limestone hills behind as we entered the path through the larch and fir plantations. Nick frequently consulted the map to make sure that we were on course for the castle. As we walked along the forest path the glare of the bright sun seemed far away. We were far from the bleating sheep and lowing cows of the sunlit fields. The hush of the woods awed us and made us feel the remoteness of the outside world. We imposed our presence on the forest by quoting bits from Batman and Peter Cook and Dudley Moore.

At last we came to a clearing. Oaks and ashes had replaced the dark conifers which marched in rows up and down the precipitous hills. On the far side of a dark tarn the ruins of the castle reared on a steep cliff.

It was Nick who broke the silence.

"Legend number one states that in the fourteenth century two armed and mounted knights of the de Pomeroy family evaded capture by riding their horses over the wall and crashing to their deaths on the rocks below. On moonless nights their ghosts re-enact their deaths according to legend."

I looked up at the jagged pinnacles of masonry and the crows and jackdaws circling above then in the azure sky.

"The ragged walls we see are evidence of the Parliamentarian cannon pounding the Royalist stronghold of the Seymours. The pillars of masonry that we see are the remains of the great hall and the long gallery which led to the kitchen block over on the right," said John.

Nick breathed hard through his nose. "We need to make a move. If we go to the left of the pond we will find a track which will take us up to the level of the castle gates," he said. "Come on lads, get fell in."

"Bollocks," I replied sourly, resenting Nick's assumption that he always had to take command and tell us what we already knew that we had to do.

"…and your bra and panties," said Henry. I added "Busty substances."

"Shut up Dud and Pete," said Nick. As we were labouring uphill, nobody argued.

We came to a level grassy space between the woods and the steep wall of the castle. We could clearly see that the Seymours had built a mansion in the middle of the de Pomeroys' defensive walls. Both castle and mansion were equally ruined and an air of melancholy lay over the whole place. Towers rose from the corners of the walls and an imposing gatehouse with twin towers seemed to be the only way in to the ruined mansion in the interior of the high walls. We were strangely reluctant to go in. We sat on the grass looking at the ramparts and at the glassless windows of the ruined mansion.

At last we got up and walked over to the gatehouse. Together we walked into the shade of the passage between the towers; we each paid our one shilling and sixpences to the custodian in the narrow room in the gatehouse. We emerged into the inner courtyard of the castle, a grassy enclosed space consisting of humps, hollows and buried stones.

Once more we sat down in a group. Charles spoke up.

"After terrible experiences in the trenches the poet Robert Graves came here for a visit with a friend from Torquay. He found the atmosphere of the castle not only terrifying but claustrophobic. He had recurrent nightmares every night and had to come back to the castle to confront his demons. He wrote a poem which he called "The Castle", full of images of torture and imprisonment. This exorcised his fear and he never came back."

"Here endeth the second lesson," said Henry quietly. A small dark cloud obscured the sun for a moment. "The Pathetic Fallacy," I remarked to no-one in particular.

We sat on the grass below the huge sightless windows of the roofless Seymour mansion. Then John spoke in his quiet and precise way.

"If you look over at the round tower at the corner of the ramparts you will see the Margaret Tower. In the time of the de Pomeroys two sisters fell in love with the same man. The elder was plain while her younger sister Margaret was beautiful. Inevitably the older sister had Margaret imprisoned in the tower, where, after a number of years, she died from a broken heart or starvation or both. If you see her ghost you will die young, so the legend has it."

Intrigued, we picked ourselves up and walked along the ramparts to the Margaret tower, where we stood in a circle. Looking at the fireplaces and the

95

holes in the walls where floors had once been I said: "There is a well documented account of a visit by a doctor in the middle of last century who was summoned to attend the wife of the estate steward whose cottage this was. The doctor came all the way from Torquay and pronounced the woman out of danger and on the road to recovery. Just before leaving he noticed a lady in the cottage standing by the fireplace. When he asked who she was the steward turned pale and murmured that his wife would die and that there was now no hope for her. The doctor took his leave unable to reassure the steward that all was well. He later found the within a few days the steward's wife had taken a turn for the worse and had died.

Perhaps this bears out my contention that anyone who sees Lady Margaret is doomed," I said with my tongue in my cheek.

We made our way back to where we had been sitting on the uneven grass in front of the Seymour mansion. I glanced up at the ramparts to see, framed in an embrasure, a girl's pale face. It was thin and pinched, the cheekbones prominent and the chin unnaturally pointed. Long dark hair framed the girl's face whose expression was both remote and sad at the same time. I blinked in surprise and looked straight back at empty air. I should have been surprised but felt inevitability in the encounter. It was as if the girl had been waiting for me.

Nick suggested that we went our separate ways within the precincts of the castle to measure, record and photograph various aspects of the domestic and defensive architecture. We willingly dispersed. It was as if we had to be alone to appreciate the remoteness of the place in which we found ourselves.

When we came together a couple of hours later I could tell by the expression on the faces of my friends that they too had seen the girl. Each was possessed by an inevitability, a tacit admission that something had happened to each of us that we could never share with each other. Quietly we left the castle in the middle of its dark forest and trudged back to Totnes through dusty and darkening lanes under a sky that was becoming thundery and oppressive. We arrived back in town with none of the usual camaraderie. Pete and Dud were forgotten and Batman was a distant memory.

As days grew into weeks and weeks grew into months and years we never came together again as a group. We seemed to retreat into ourselves and things were never the same again. We studied for our A levels and were generally successful.

Henry was the first to die. After many years teaching at King Edward VI he went foxhunting one Saturday. The master of the Dart Vale and Haldon

Harriers found him in a ditch with a broken neck. The inquest found that he had broken his neck falling from a high bank while following the hounds. A verdict of accidental death was the matter laid to rest except in the minds of his friends.

Next to die was Nick. Major Nick Tozer was killed by a round to the head on Tumbledown Mountain in the Falklands. The bullet was a 7.62 high velocity round and could have been fired by an Argie of by one of ours. Nick was, of course, buried with full military honours. Charles's death was more unexpected. He found a distraught man in his church in Leeds one evening. He tried to help him, but the man pulled out a knife and stabbed him through the heart. Charles died instantly and the man was found to be hopelessly insane and committed to an asylum for the rest of his life.

John was killed by a car while crossing the road at the traffic lights by his house. The driver of the car said at his trial that a woman's voice had been urging him to crash the red light. He was ordered to receive psychiatric help. John was cremated at Torquay Crematorium with many of his friends and acquaintances in the congregation.

I am the only one left and the only one of the five who has made it into his fifties. The dreams keep coming. The girl is always there, beckoning. I cannot tell if the look on her face is sweet or greedy. Last week I went to the Leatside Surgery. Dr Killock told me gravely that my heart is dangerously diseased. I am experiencing increasing chest pains and the pain in my right arm is getting worse. Perhaps I should consider cancelling the sponsored cycle ride over Dartmoor this weekend. I'm sure that English Heritage would prefer a live member to a dead sponsor…

Private Angove

I count it one of the great blessings of my life that I was able to take early retirement and move to St Perrans when I did. The village was quite far from a main road and clustered around its ancient church with its tall trees echoing to the raucous call of rooks. From the centre of the village narrow lanes wandered in all directions to cross other lanes in the lush wooded landscape. St Perrans lay in a fold of the hills away from the salty winds of the north coast and seemed, at first sight, to be quite idyllic. In the shadow of the grey church tower cottages clustered on a network of short streets. The village shop, Primary School and pub gave life to the place where most of the families were still local.

Tragedy had visited the village on a number of occasions. Nine names were engraved on a slate tablet set on the high church wall; ten men from the parish had served in the Great War, either in France or Belgium or on the freezing waters of the North Atlantic. One name had been erased from the monument. At the head of the list was a blank just above Corporal Barnicoat. I reckoned that the man's name had probably begun with an A and made a mental note to find out why a name had been incised later to be removed.

I settled easily into my small cottage on the edge of the village. It was squat and low, crouching behind a stone hedge with only the first floor windows visible. The interior was snug and roomy in a way that only Cornish cottages can be. The garden was extensive and suitable for growing vegetables and all manner of flowers. On one granite gatepost was an old hand painted sign with the cottage's name *Chy an gof.* Not being very proficient in the Cornish language I consulted Nance's dictionary to find out that my house had been the home of the village blacksmiths for many years. Perhaps that explained the profusion of horseshoes that I dug up in my expanding vegetable patch.

I soon found a number of other objects in the soil, coins, nails, fragments of china and buttons. I loved working the soil; the dark loam was deep and fragrant and was soon cleared of roots. As spring broke in the hedges and trees all round me I felt very much a part of the village.

One day I asked Mrs Williams in the Post Office who had previously lived in my house. Her face darkened at the thought as she told me about the

Angove family who had lived there ever since anyone could remember. She was normally a pleasant woman and I was surprised at the change in her features.

"Those Angoves were strange folk. We never could get on with them, in fact we grew to hate them. It wasn't so much what they did but how they were. They died out after the disgrace in the First World War. I suppose that there were no longer any male Angove left to carry on the line so the house became vacant and has changed hands a number of times since," she said.

"What was the 'disgrace' Mrs Williams?" I asked.

"I would rather not speak ill of the dead, Mr Hoskins. If you live here any length of time you'll find out soon enough," she replied.

Firmly put in my place I walked home. At least I had a name to go on and now I was determined to research the history of the Angove family. I stopped in front of the War Memorial tablet. Of course! The name that had been erased was obviously a surname beginning with A. I was almost certain that it could have been Angove.

Next day I had some shopping to do in Bodmin and, having found my way there with only one wrong turning, I walked past the station to the imposing granite barracks that housed the Duke of Cornwall's Light Infantry Museum. Once inside I was fascinated by the numerous exhibits, particularly those from the First World War. I found it strange that so many young Cornish men had volunteered to go to the trenches. Times were hard and employment not easy to find. I was haunted by the young faces that gazed out of the faded photographs from France and Belgium, young men, many below average height, encumbered with helmets, rifles, bayonets, gas masks and all manner of awkward kit. Many of the men looked desperate and tired, a few downright scared, but all revealed a dogged determination which was touching in the extreme. Tentatively I approached the elderly man in the DCLI tie behind the counter and asked him about a soldier named Angove.

"Well Sir, and what would be your connection to that man? We don't have many enquiries about Private Angove, seeing that it is rather a touchy part of the Regiment's history," he said, looking at me rather sadly and seriously.

"I live in his house in St Perrans," I replied. What was I getting myself into, I wondered.

"I regret to tell you that Private Angove, Second Battalion, DCLI, was shot for desertion in the face of the enemy on July 2nd 1916 in the early stages of the Battle of the Somme. His name was put in error on the war memorial at St Perrans but was later removed," I was quietly told.

Thanking the custodian I quickly left and walked down the steep street to the public library. Once inside I sat down in front of a computer and typed in "Private Angove, DCLI, WW1". Angoves from the length and breadth of Cornwall came up on the screen in front of me. Sure enough, there was a Private Thomas Angove executed for cowardice in 1916. He was from the Third Battalion and I was sure that the man at the museum had said that he was from the Second Battalion.

The photograph showed a stocky, heavily moustached man with bright eyes and an aggressive demeanour. Not a man to be crossed or trifled with, I thought. I wondered how long he had been in the line before he snapped. Perhaps he had been shell shocked and had wandered, dazed, in the wrong direction to be picked up by some behind-the-lines Military Policeman. I felt great sympathy for the man even though he was the type of man I would not have taken to in real life. I found it hard to think of that man living in my house and going off to die in France.

Back home I shook off the negative feelings caused by my visit to Bodmin. I could save the rest of the afternoon. The sun was shining and the garden was a riot of birdsong, so I changed into my gardening clothes and took my Cornish shovel, known as a Devon spade where I come from, out of the shed to the vegetable plot. Partly enclosed by high grassy banks, the plot had been cleared of all surface weeds and was ready to be turned. I started at the bottom by digging a deep trench and dug steadily in rows, heaving and turning the dark clods without having to bend at all except to pick out roots and the occasional stone. I wondered if I would find any artefacts apart from the horseshoes that had lain just below the surface when I mattocked off the rough turf.

After an hour's work I had developed a rhythm which was pleasant and made me feel truly alive. Strange how the thought of digging was far worse than the actual labour of it. I turned up what appeared to be a miniature horseshoe but was a heel plate from a hobnailed boot. I placed it on a flat stone along with a halfpenny from the reign of George V and a glass marble. It would be interesting to keep all my finds and even display them together at some point. Just when I was deciding to go inside and call it a day, just as the shadows were lengthening and the first chill was cooling the sweat on my face, I saw what appeared to be a brooch lying on the surface of the soil. I picked it up and rubbed it, making out the word "Cornwall" on its surface. A souvenir brooch, I wondered; then recognised it with a slight shock of surprise.

A curved horn over the word "Cornwall" took me back to the museum I had visited in Bodmin that very day. What a coincidence: the grimy object I held in my hand was a brass cap badge from the Duke of

Cornwall's Light Infantry! I cleaned it carefully with soap and an old toothbrush, nothing abrasive, and found its blackened brass very similar to the badges from the First World War that I had seen in Bodmin. I wondered if this one had belonged to Private Angove. If so how could he have been so careless as to lose it in the garden?

After more research on the internet I found that the horn on the badge was in fact a bugle, the symbol of all light infantry regiments. These regiments had been formed in the Peninsula War in the early 1800s as an early form of commandos. Lightly armed and very fit, the soldiers of light infantry regiments were used in reconnaissance and fighting patrol roles. They were the eyes and ears of the army as well as dependable riflemen. They were elite troops and served with distinction in many theatres of war. The Duke of Cornwall's Light Infantry had a proud and distinguished record.

Next day dawned bright and hazy and I was determined to dig the rest of the vegetable plot. The church clock struck eight as I pulled on my wellingtons and set off for the bottom of the garden with my spade in my hand. After a few minutes the stiffness eased out of my arms and back and I bent to pick up a dome shaped object turned up by my spade. It was an army button with the shape of the curved bugle emerging in relief from the dark soil clinging to it.

It appeared that I was building up a collection of DCLI insignia.

Imagine my delight when up came another brass button and a brass shoulder title with the word CORNWALL shining dully from the soil. One more button completed the day's finds as well as pieces of clay pipe and a tarnished Victorian farthing.

The day's digging forgotten; I carefully cleaned my finds and went straight to the computer in my study. I found that a DCLI infantryman of the First World War would have worn a rough khaki serge jacket with four patch pockets, loose woollen trousers with puttees wound up the knees, hobnailed boots with thirteen nails in each sole and a peaked stiffened serge cap which was replaced in 1916 by a steel helmet in the trenches. What was altogether more interesting was that each cap sported a regimental cap badge at the front and that, on the jacket, there were five large brass buttons and two smaller ones on the flaps of the top pockets. On the two shoulder straps were two curving brass shoulder titles and on the tops of the lapels two regimental collar dogs. Was it possible that I would find the whole set and, if I did, what would it tell me about the late Private Angove?

Next morning, with the rooks cawing in the tall churchyard trees, I set to work again in the vegetable garden. I was oblivious to the sound of people passing and of farm traffic roaring noisily by. I had two aims: to complete the digging of the vegetable patch and to find the rest of Private Angove's misplaced insignia.

By lunchtime I had all five tunic buttons and one collar dog. Most of the patch was dug and I hoped that I could find the stamina to keep going. After lunch up came one more collar dog and one of the tiny pocket buttons. I retired for the night aching and stiff and slept soundly.

The next day was fortunately fine and I was determined to complete both tasks awaiting me at the bottom of the garden. By the end of the day I had dug the whole patch and had all the insignia and buttons apart from one shoulder title. I was very pleased and determined to go back to Bodmin on the following day to find out why the insignia of a man who died in France could have ended up at the bottom of my garden.

That night I found it hard to fall asleep. I was excited by the thought that a mystery could soon be solved even though I had no idea how. I finally fell asleep in the early hours of the morning only to come bolt awake as a beam of bright moonlight fell directly across my face. I was aware that there was someone in the shadows in the corner of my room. I sat up and called out in a shaky voice, "Who goes there? Reveal yourself!"

In the colourless moonlight a small man in a filthy khaki uniform emerged from the shadows. I knew that he was not alive but felt no fear, only a sense of wonder. The man held a field cap in his right hand and took a hesitant step towards me. I could clearly see the filthy puttees wound tightly up to the knees of his trousers. His dark eyes gazed intensely into mine and I realised, with a shock, that he wore no heavy moustache. He was clearly not the Private Angove whose photograph I had seen in Bodmin.

A smile of recognition and delight lit up his pale young face. I understood now exactly what I had to do.

Next morning I phoned the DCLI museum in Bodmin and made an appointment with the Director. I collected my insignia and shut and locked the front door of the cottage behind me as I set out once again. A dull object gleamed from a flower bed and I had found the missing shoulder title.

Once safely inside the museum I was shown courteously into the Director's office. Colonel Bolitho listened intently to my story and then carefully replied.

"You ask how the insignia of a man who was executed in France could have turned up all those years later in the garden of his former home. We clearly have here a case of mistaken identity. Private Angove of the Second Battalion and Private Angove of the Third Battalion were two different men. I did some research of my own after your phone call this morning. The two Angoves were cousins; one was shot while the other returned home to your cottage at the end of the war. The records were later confused as Thomas Angove of St Perrans soon moved away to St Teath where his late cousin had lived.

Thank you for setting the record straight. It is probable that Thomas Angove moved away from his home because of the reputation of his cousin and that the records of the two men were deliberately mixed up by people who did not like the family."

I had not told the Colonel about my night time visitation. I agreed with what he said but had one more question for him.

"Why, then, did I find all the insignia and buttons in the soil, given that Angove returned home?" I asked.

"That's easy to answer. At the end of the war returning soldiers were allowed to keep their service uniforms. As they wore out, they were usually burned in the garden in the days before regular rubbish collections. The buttons and badges remained in the soil. They were rarely prized and were allowed to disappear along with the fading memories of the war."

"I can understand that. Thank you for your solution to Private Angove's problem. I now have two things to do which won't be particularly easy for an outsider."

With a heavy heart I drove home again. I wondered how long St Perrans would continue to be my home. I need not have worried; Mrs Williams at the Post Office was moved to tears by my story and was willing to lay at last the family feud to rest. She had not realised that there were in fact two Private Angoves and felt terrible that an untruth of several generations ago had been carried up to the present.

At the next Parish Council meeting I stood before the councillors, two of whom were named Williams, and explained why Thomas Angove's name should be put back onto the War Memorial. After due consideration and a short discussion the matter was unanimously approved. I returned home to my cottage with a new sense of peace.

<u>Young Harry</u>

Bodmin lay under a grey pall of drizzle, its granite walls and slate roofs slick and dully shining under a sickly moon. The High Street was deserted, the GWR terminus quiet. Most windows were squares of darkness; only the occasional pane revealed wan lamplight within.

The vast bulk of the gaol reared on the northern edge of the silent town. High up one of the granite walls faint gaslight glowed from behind a barred aperture. Above the still town sat Selena Wadge in the condemned cell. She was quiet and composed as she leaned forward to speak to Dr Quiller-Couch, physician to the County Prison, Bodmin.

"I'm not afeared to die tomorrow if it will rid me of the Devil's spawn. I don't welcome the pain of death, but I deserve to die. I pray that God will deliver my soul from the hell that I've lived these last two years.

I was born near Launceston and brought up in the workhouse. Life was hard and no one showed me any affection. I worked hard and was fed and clothed in rags at the town's expense. I was trained for service and worked hard for my masters at the big house. For a while I was reasonably happy but the young master took advantage of me and I fell pregnant. I went back to the Lanson workhouse and bore the babe, my young John, who is presently being cared for by a good couple in the town who will bring him up to be a God-fearing man who, unlike his mother, will have no further truck with the Devil.

Johnny and I were given a second chance at Altarnun, on the edge of the moor. We were housed at the Grange and I went back into service. All went well for three years. Then I met Mr Dewer, a friend of the master's. Mr Dewer would come up to the Grange and drink and play cards on many nights of the week. He paid me mind and oft times spoke kindly to me.

One evening he arrived early at the Grange and sat talking to me while he waited for Master to come in from a day with the hounds. He asked me if I was happy and what I would do to improve my life. I told him that I would do almost anything to be respected and independent, having grown up in such dire circumstances. He looked at me long and hard and told me that my chance could come sooner than I thought. I told him that I didn't know what he meant but he just looked at me with a slow twinkle in his eye.

He looked away as the master came in all mired up and in a filthy temper.

The upshot of the evening's cards was that I became the property of Mr Dewer for the night. I must admit that I didn't mind too much because he was kind and treated me a sight better than any man before or since. By his actions I fell pregnant once more and was put away for a third time in the Lanson workhouse. The pregnancy was long and hard. I was constantly sick and was nearly dead by the month that my time had come. In great pain and despair I was delivered of a boy, but a boy quite unlike my dear little Johnny.

It was as if Harry, for that was his name, had drained all the strength and the goodness out of me. He was a large child and a very lazy one who showed me no affection nor the least consideration. Nothing I could do for him was enough. He would look at me with those slitted goat's eyes and snarl. He could never be content unless he was wearing me down or bending me to his selfish will. And as he grew, his fat body grew wiry black hair…"

"Calm yourself, Miss Wadge," said the Doctor. "Do not distress yourself; the Lord's will be done…"

Selena drew herself upright. She was a tall woman, prematurely aged by the hard life she had lived. She was not unattractive with her long dark hair and pale forehead. Had circumstances been different, thought the Doctor, she could have lived happily as the wife of a farmer or craftsman.

Dr Quiller-Couch could not help thinking that her slender neck would be three or four inches longer by this time tomorrow.

"'Twas but a few months ago that I met Mr Jenkin. It was he who befriended me. He would walk all the way from Bude nearly to Lanson just to visit with me. He treated me with respect and never presumed to lay a hand on me. He was some sort of minister of religion in a part-time sort of way.

Harry couldn't abide him. When Mr Jenkin visited, Harry would growl and snarl at him and spit if he was within range. As the child grew, it became apparent that his feet were in some way deformed. They seemed to be splitting, with three toes growing out one way and two the other. Of course he wasn't able to walk at all and had to be carried everywhere we went.

When he were above one year old, Harry began to talk. His voice was harsh and sounded more like a gook than a child. He began to shout out filthy words such as he could never have heard from either Mr Jenkin or myself. When he said these words he would laugh; it were the only time he ever did so. He showed no love of affection to anyone. He would just demand to be fed and watered, clothed and amused. If he were impatient or crossed in any way he would curse and blaspheme, his yellow eyes would narrow and light up.

A couple of months ago Mr Jenkin sent me a postcard from Bude to say that he would meet me in a field just north of Lanson on such and such a day in the afternoon. I welcomed his visit and set out to meet him carrying Harry in a cloth on my hip. As I left the houses of the town behind me, I could feel Harry's twisted toes digging into my side like hard little hooves. From time to time he would foul himself, making no attempt not to do so. I cleaned and changed him every time without a murmur. I was determined to be as good a mother to this child as was humanly possible.

In a short time I reached a large windswept field at Botathen with a boarded-over well in one corner and a few bent thorn bushes in the hedge opposite. I was wary of this field because it was the one where the ghost of Dorothy Dingley walked near two hundred years ago. She would appear to a boy on his way to school and drift along beside him until he left the field. On occasions she even attempted to block his way.

I saw a figure rise up in front of me but 'twas only Mr Jenkin. He gave me a bunch of wild flowers and we sat down on a bank beside the old well. I put Harry down to crawl around on his cloth. As soon as I turned to talk to Mr Jenkin, Harry began to talk. In a deep voice he said: "Jenkin, you bastard, you filthy scum!" and terms very much worse that I will not permit to pass my lips. He then crouched on his crippled feet and shouted "*an jawl!*" in a piercing voice.

At this Mr Jenkin turned white and pointed at Harry with a shaking finger.

"He said Satan's filthy name in the old language. Look at him! He is indeed the Devil's spawn. He has become so through no fault of yours! He is not fit to live. We must destroy him before he destroys us. As he grows and becomes stronger he will take us over and we shall be ensnared by his father the Devil. We must act now and may a merciful God have mercy on our souls!"

As Mr Jenkin said these terrible words Harry did urinate and drop his dung upon the cloth. He was chuckling as I snatched him up and farted loud and long as I carried him over to the well shaft. Mr Jenkin pulled off the some of the rotten planks and I flung the foul creature wailing down the well. There was a splash as he entered the water, a few seconds churning around and then merciful silence.

We were both mightily shaken by what we had done and sat for some time in silence. Then we went on our separate ways and I have not heard since from Mr Jenkin. Indeed no trace of him could be found in Bude or Stratton, nor anywhere up by the north coast.

So I come to be here. I cannot deny that I killed Harry but would do it again for the peace it has brought me, even here in the condemned cell. I feel that God will have mercy on me but that I must pay the price for what I have done to rid the world of the Devil's child."

Dr Quiller-Couch sighed deeply. He patted Selena's arm.

"In the morning you will have a chance to talk to the chaplain. I will tell him in confidence what you have told me. You will pray together before you go to your rest. I have every confidence that God will pardon you and take you into Paradise."

"Thank you Doctor for listening to me. Now please leave me. I must pray and sleep a little to prepare myself for the morrow."

As he quietly left the cell the doctor turned down the gaslight. Selina turned her face to the wall and said her prayers. Presently she drifted off into a deep sleep. Her dreams were confused and oppressive. Just before dawn her head cleared and she saw, as if suspended in the air near the stained ceiling of her cell, the radiant figure of her son Harry. He was standing on his feet and his eyes were blue and clear. He smiled down as his mother as she awoke to the last day of her life.

Selena Wadge was hanged at noon on September 15th 1878. A canvas sheet was suspended in front of the open-fronted execution shed to make her death more private. As the trap was sprung and dropped open she died instantly with hardly a twitch. Her body hung for a while above the brick pit, a white handkerchief gripped in her right hand. Her last words were: "Thank God it's nearly over…"

Sir Cloudesley

"Hurry, Sir, hurry, 'tis old Mrs Thomas. She's a dying on the other side of the island. She must see you avore the spirit leaves her."

With a deep sigh, the Reverend Septimus Ough, Chaplain to the Isles of Scilly, took down his heavy burial cloak from the peg by the front door of the parsonage house. It was the autumn of 1750 and the island of St Mary's was strangely hushed. The wind that normally blew through the sparse trees of the garden had dropped and a new moon shone high and remote in the starry sky. Reverend Ough saddled his horse with the distant crash of the sea on the beach behind him. He felt the chill of winter approaching, the days and nights of howling gales and flying spume ahead of him.

He had quite a long ride ahead of him. Mrs Thomas's turf thatched cottage lay across the island from Hugh Town on the far western side of the island, the most remote and backward part of a poverty stricken pocket of land on the Atlantic's edge. Most people there lived by subsistence farming and by the sea. The Hugh Town folk said that the westerners still lured ships onto the rocks and beaches at night to plunder their cargos and crews.

Parson Ough rode past groups of elm trees and small walled fields. He reigned in his horse as the land began to slope westwards to the gleaming shore. The few trees thinned out and became twisted and stunted by the salt wind. He made out a small low building almost enclosed by a turf bank not far from the curved white strand that formed St Mary's western edge. The tiny moon hung in the sky, its reflected image shimmering on the rippled sea.

The parson dismounted and tied his horse to a bent thorn bush which grew out of the bank enclosing Mrs Thomas's vegetable garden. He opened the driftwood gate and walked the few steps to the low door of the cottage. A feeble voice called out to him to "Come you in."

Inside the low ceilinged room he took off his cloak and let his eyes adjust to the glimmering candlelight. The room was whitewashed and clean, sparse and scrubbed. In one corner an ancient lady sat up in in her bed, her wasted body wrapped in a tartan shawl. Wispy grey hair straggled over a creased face. Eyes bright with fever sought the parson's eyes and a withered brown hand clasped his.

"Parson Ough, I've done a wrong, a very great wrong, the burden of it I must share with you before I give up my soul," she whispered, her voice as soft as the sea billows. Ough recognised the old lilt peculiar to the islands and, sitting on a chair hard by the bed, bent down to catch the old woman's feeble words.

"'Twas in the autumn of 1707 that I lost my dear Jack, the only man I ever loved or who loved me. He was an Able Seaman in Her Majesty's Royal Navy and a St Mary's man, born and bred just to the south of here. He was proud to sail to the Mediterranean on the *Association*, Rear Admiral Sir Cloudesley Shovell's flagship, to teach the Frenchies a thing or two. After the siege of Toulon the fleet set sail via Gibraltar to return home.

In the October of that year I knew the fleet was fast approaching the Scillies. I have the second sight passed down to me from my mother and sometimes I see visions. On the afternoon of the 20th I was raking up kelp from the beach not far from this house when I heard a long wail coming from far out of the western sea. It was Jack's voice. When his cry was cut off I knew that he was dead. I had a vision of his body hanging stark from one of the mainmast yards and I saw the awful fat figure of Sir Cloudesley in lace cuffs and powdered wig wave his arm to order my poor dead Jack cut down. And I knew that all this was taking place just a few miles over the western horizon.

The fleet had sailed for days in a terrible fog, had been becalmed and had lost their way. Because they had no reliable timepiece they were unable to work out their longitude. Sir Cloudesley reckoned that they were as far south as Ushant off the coast of Brittany. Jack smelled the burning kelp and knew the fleet were dangerously close to the shores of the Scillies and told the Admiral that they were in great danger. For this presumption Sir Cloudesley had him court martialled and hanged before the whole crew of the *Association.* His body was wrapped in his hammock, weighted with ballast and dumped into the sea. For this act I felt true hatred for the first and last time in my life.

The 22nd October was a fair day with a clear sky and a brisk wind from the west, an onshore breeze. I felt cast down and oppressed all day and when I saw the sails of the fleet on the horizon in the evening I felt no lifting of the spirits. Led by the *Association,* the fleet drove straight onto the rocks of the Scillies.

I saw the flagship go onto the Gilstone Rock not fifty yards from here. Even with sails taken in she was unable to turn or to stop. With a rending crash she went onto the ledges and was soon a total loss. Her masts fell in a tangle of spars and sail and every man on board was cast into the surf and lost except for one. I saw the bodies come ashore and I was glad that my Jack was already gone to his maker.

Another ship grounded close to the *Association* but a freak wave lifted her off again and she made her way back to the open sea. Two other ships were wrecked nearby and close to two thousand sailors lost. Their bodies and bits of their bodies were cast up on shore for weeks afterwards. We had to go and try to identify the men and then bury their remains hard by the shore.

The morning after the wreck I was down at Porthellic Cove to glean what I could from the wreck. Times were hard and we had to live the best we could. I walked along the strand until I came to the body of a fat man cast ashore. I bent down to look at him and saw that he still breathed. I saw that he wore lace at his sleeve and that his wig had been washed away. Then I knew that he was the Admiral, Sir Cloudesley Shovell himself, and that he had ordered the death of my dear Jack. A cold fury took hold of me and I bent down to smother the bastard. He shook and he shivered but I was too strong for him and, with a shudder, he died. In a rage I took the two rings from his blue and swollen fingers and I cast him into the ebb tide to drift away to eternity as far as I cared.

I know now that I have done a great wrong and I repent of my sins. May God find it in His heart to have mercy on my soul. One of the rings I sold many years ago but the other I have kept and will deliver it to you this eve.

Parson Ough, go you to the press in the corner of the room and you will find Sir Cloudesley's ring. Take it and return it to his family wrapped in a scrap of paper with the name *Jack Sherris* inscribed thereon. Offer no explanation but pray for the souls of Sir Cloudesley Shovell and Mary Thomas. May the great God have eternal mercy on our souls."

The old lady slumped down into her bed and turned her face to the wall. Her breathing became shallow and laboured as Parson Ough recited the Lord's Prayer and the prayer for the dead. He gave absolution to the recumbent figure of Mary Thomas as her life slipped away and anointed her forehead with holy oil.

The small room had become unbearably hot. Parson Ough stood up and opened the small casement on the seaward side of the cottage. He looked out onto the starlit strand to see two figures standing side by side on the glistening sand. He could not make out the details of their features but saw that one man was fat and stocky and the other tall and lean with his head tilted at an unnatural angle. He watched while the figures gradually faded away and then turned to Mary Thomas's bedside. He saw the thin chest rise and fall for the last time and then all was still and peaceful. Darkness entered the mouth of Mary Thomas and remained there.

It remained to Parson Ough to open the door of the corner cupboard and search diligently. At last he found a fat gold ring with an amethyst set in diamonds. It gleamed in the candlelight and weighed heavy in his hand. Such wealth would transform the little church at Hugh Town and enable great works to be done on behalf of the islanders.

But no: Parson Ough had given his word that the ring would be sent back to the family of Sir Cloudesley. And thus it was accomplished; the truth was out and the Chaplaincy of the Isles of Scilly received a modest emolument. Now both Mary Thomas and Sir Cloudesley lay peacefully in their graves, united by the democracy of death.

Vade mecum

Once again I entered the vast enclosed space of the church of St Mary Magdalene in Launceston. For the last twenty years I had been drawn there by an attraction I could not describe.   There were finer churches in Cornwall, St Nonna's in Alternun for instance, but St Mary's drew me back like an old friend, familiar and intimate.

I closed the heavy door behind me and looked up at the barrel vaulted roof high above, dust motes swirling in the late afternoon sunlight. I took in the ordered ranks of pews, the battle flags hanging dustily at the back of the church and the fine monument to the Wise family with its stone ranks of children. My eyes moved to the fine screen and choir stalls, finally to the high altar and heavy reredos. Inevitably my attention was drawn to the south aisle, to the monuments not far from the massive door.

Between two colourful Victorian windows, one of which commemorated the Ching family, were two white marble plaques, one scrolled and ornate, the other small and plain to the point of starkness, a marked contrast to the other more demonstrative tablets on the walls of the church.

I sat down in a pew a few feet from the plain tablet. I would wait a little before reading it even though I knew by heart the plain words inscribed into its surface. I relaxed in the pew remembering the first time I had visited the church.

Nearly forty years earlier my friend Titch and I had embarked on a cycle tour of north Cornwall. We had set off from our homes near Totnes to cross the Moor, eventually arriving exhausted at the Tavistock youth hostel. Next day we had eventually crossed the Tamar into Cornwall and ridden up the long, steep hill into Launceston. With a great sense of accomplishment we had entered the hilltop town through its Southgate, parking our bikes outside an ancient pub. After a look at the town and its castle rising remote on its mound we enjoyed excellent fish and chips and went to the church to shelter from a squall of heavy rain.

We had sat in the pew in which I now sat, plucking up courage to begin the long ride up to St Stephens and on through isolated byways to the coast at Boscastle. The angry rain had spattered the high windows as we sat in the warm gloom. We would have happily stayed the rest of the day and all night in

St Mary's just to avoid the effort of a wet and windy ride along miles of lanes to the Atlantic coast.

And so, inevitably, my eyes sought the words on the memorial tablet. I read them slowly, even though I had no real need to do so.

IN MEMORY OF

THOMAS PROCKTER CHING

YOUNGEST SON OF THE ABOVE

AGED 22 WHO, IN THE MONTH OF AUGUST 1834

AFTER HAVING BEEN WRECKED

IN THE SHIP "CHARLES EATON" ON A VOYAGE TO CHINA

SUFFERED A MORE CRUEL FATE

AT THE HANDS OF IGNORANT SAVAGES,

BY WHOM THE CREW WERE DECOYED AND MURDERED

IN THE ISLAND OF BOYDANG IN TORRES STRAITS.

Once again I found myself wondering what had happened to the unfortunate Ching. Had he indeed been killed by 'savages'? Had they eaten him? Were they 'ignorant'? Why had they killed him? Such questions were bound to remain unanswered when interpreted by a grief-stricken family who had no knowledge of the life of the Torres Straits islanders. Perhaps I should research the lives and beliefs of the natives of the islands that lay between Australia and New Guinea.

But, in the end, why should I bother? Why was I so affected by a monument to a young man who died in a remote corner of the barely explored world so long ago? The world has turned so many times since the reign of William IV so why dig up ground left fallow for so long?

I was aware of the presence of someone just behind my left shoulder. I slowly turned to see a young man standing with his hands clasped in front of him. He was pale and earnest, of slight stature. Indeed his presence seemed not to disturb the peace of the church at all.

At last he spoke:

"Excuse me, but I see you are reading the monument of Thomas Ching. I have studied the life and death of that man and may be of assistance in any research that you might undertake. Allow me to help you in any way that I can."

I looked fully at the young man. He was of less than average height and seemed to be of a studious turn of mind. He was probably in his early twenties and either in his last year at university or embarking on a post graduate course of higher education.

My curiosity was aroused. I would use the resources offered by my young friend and find out more about the fate of Thomas Ching.

"I appreciate your kind offer and would very much like to learn more about Ching. Thank you very much for your timely appearance," I replied.

"Please come with me. I will show you some of the places associated with the Ching family," said the young man. "By the way, my name is Tom and I'm from Launceston."

I recognised that the burr of his voice was local and followed him up the three steps into the church porch where we stood on the cobbled half-circle across the road from the bookshop. Tom pointed to a number of granite grave slabs immediately to the left of the porch.

"These are the tombs of the later Chings, the brothers, sisters and uncles of Thomas Ching. The family had a great influence on the town in Queen Victoria's reign but have now died out."

He pointed to a Celtic cross with a number of leaden names set into it. "The last of the Chings in Lanson was Lawrence Ching who died in 1915 after a life at sea."

We walked on up the narrow twisting street. Tom showed me the house in Broad Street where Thomas had grown up and where his family had prospered long after his early death. He walked me round the corner to Southgate Street to show me the Georgian house that had become Ching's Wine Vaults later in the century of his death. He showed me the White Hart Inn which had been once owned by Thomas's grandfather and from where he had embarked on a number of long journeys and voyages.

Tom was a quiet companion, undemanding but insistent that he show me everything that he knew about the Ching family. As the clock in the tall church tower struck seven and as the shadows lengthened in the streets of the hilltop town Tom led me to the green in front of the castle. A glorious view of tumbled houses and small fields rising to wooded hilltops stretched in front of us dusted by the rays of the sinking red orb to the west. I felt a great emptiness: it was true that I had learned a great deal about Thomas Ching but I felt that there was so much more almost within my reach.

"This was the view that Thomas remembered when he was at sea and when he thought of home. He always came here when he was about to leave home and when he returned safely from a long voyage," said Tom in a soft voice.

My curiosity was aroused. "How could you possibly know that? Did Thomas leave a diary or letters?" I asked a little sharply, instantly regretting my hasty words.

"Thomas left no diary and no letters have survived. But I know it to be true," replied my earnest companion.

"I'm sorry to have spoken so hastily," I replied. "Let me take you to The White Hart for some supper. I should like to ask you some more questions about Thomas Ching. You have been more than generous with your time and your information. It is the least that I can do…"

"Thank you kindly, but there is one place to which we must return before we finish. Please come back to the church with me."

Tom led the way through dusky streets around the shadowed bulk of the castle. We walked silently down a slight hill to the church porch and down into the church. I sat in the pew nearest to Thomas Ching's tablet which seemed to glow in the dusky light. Tom stood silently beside me. I turned to look at him. As I did so he seemed to change from a modern young man in a sweat shirt and jeans to a man in the ragged clothes of a sailor. His face remained the same while his hair grew long and lank and the stubble of an untidy beard covered his hollow cheeks. Was it my imagination or could I hear the thunder of the long waves on a distant coral reef? I had the impression of ragged palm leaves somewhere over my head. I was still in the darkening church but I now knew exactly who my companion was.

He spoke again: "You must write down the story of what happened to us. Those men who killed us were not savages, nor were they ignorant. You must read the account of Ireland the cabin boy. He knows the truth. All I can do is wander, hoping to influence someone who cares…"

"Stay, please stay here. I am beginning to understand…"

Thomas Ching had begun to fade. My anguished voice brought him back. He stood, now a pitifully emaciated figure standing in the south aisle. He looked at me with an intense look of entreaty and, with a great effort, spoke again. I heard his faint words as I sat in the pew in the darkening church.

"When we came from the sea the islanders thought that we were the wayward ghosts of their ancestors. They killed us and ate parts of us to honour our souls and to set us on the right paths towards the light. We were white and adrift so they did the only thing they could for us. It took a lot of courage and resolve but it left us earthbound and isolated. We need the understanding and prayers of many people to forgive these people and set us free."

I looked hard at the slight figure of Thomas Ching standing before me in the dusk. His face was changing again, beginning to glow. I noticed with horror that the side of his face was crusted with dried blood and that in place of his eyes were pools of darkness from which more blood had oozed. Strips of his cheeks were flayed from below the empty eye sockets and his thin body had faded into the darkness. For a few seconds the glowing head hung before me in the air, then it too faded away.

I was left with the words: "Forgive them, they knew not what they did" echoing in my head. I closed my eyes, now knowing what the islanders had done to Ching. I resolved to write his story and to put it into the context of the islands. Feeling no fear but a great sadness I sat on in the dark church. A burden had been passed to me which I now fully shared and was determined to pass on in the form of the book that I was compelled to research and write.

A harsh grating sound made me rise out of the pew in a panic. Heavy footsteps crashed down the steps into the church. A cheery voice said: "Now Sir, I must shut up and lock the church before it gets much darker. I'm sorry to have startled you; you started up just as if you had seen a ghost…"

Cutty Dyer

Since early childhood Alan Dyer was haunted by a morbid fear of trolls. He had never come close to seeing one of the hairy evil-smelling miniature ogres but hated even the idea of their tenuous existence. He had no idea where his fear originated; as a lecturer in English literature he had read widely and deeply on the subject but had reached no firm conclusion as to why the thought of trolls terrified him.

Most of the time trolls were no problem in his everyday existence. Weeks and months passed with no reference to them. Then a chance encounter with a folk tale or legend froze Alan's blood and gave him sleepless nights.

Fortunately trolls were far from Alan's mind when he visited Ashburton on a drear December Saturday during the winter vacation. He was keen to spend time in the second hand bookshop searching for old editions of Poe and critical essays of his *Tales of Mystery and Imagination*. Although the shop was cold, Alan was absorbed in his examination of "tomes of half forgotten lore"

The bookshop consisted of a tall, narrow house in Kingsbridge Lane which backed onto the deep channel of a small river that rushed behind the ancient houses before diving under the main street. Every room of the house was filled with books on various subjects, all arranged in order on spindly shelves. The floors of the small rooms sloped this way and that. Most were covered with faded and dusty rugs and heated by ancient electric heaters which failed miserably in their aim of taking the chill off the still air of the chambers. Even the crooked stairs groaned under their burden of books: old Penguins, the crime novels of Edgar Wallace, a biography of Alistair Crowley.

Alan, muffled in his tweed winter coat, was totally absorbed in his quest for books on Poe. He had already found an early edition of the *Tales*, published in Baltimore at around the time of Poe's untimely death. The price was reasonable, so Alan asked the bookseller to put it on her desk while he looked for more treasures.

On the way upstairs Alan paused to look at a faded postcard in a small frame. He could just make out a doggerel verse and was intrigued to see that it concerned someone who shared his name. With difficulty he read:

Don't 'ee go down riverside
Cutty Dyer do abide
Cutty Dyer, he's no good
Cutty Dyer'll drink your blood.

No prize for poetry. Alan wondered where the verse came from. On closer inspection he saw the faint words *Ashburton 1913* in the right hand corner of the card. As to who Cutty Dyer was, Alan was fairly happy for that to remain a mystery.

After another half hour's perusal Alan was ready to leave. He was happy with the bundle of books he had found and took them carefully back to his car which he had parked in the space in front of the bookshop.

Wrapped warmly in his old tweed coat Alan turned and walked over a little hump-backed bridge that spanned the raging stream that rushed behind the bookshop and other tall old houses. He shivered a little as he turned into North Street and looked for the sign indicating Foale's Passage and the barber's shop. Sleet was beginning to fall and the cold sky had taken on a dirty yellow tinge. An east wind was blowing up the street whirling ice crystals in Alan's face.

The barber's shop was warm and welcoming. Alan brushed the sleet from his coat as he sat down to wait for his turn. The hollow wind moaned in the passage outside as Alan began to feel the warmth seeping back. He read the *Western Morning News* as he waited to have his hair trimmed.

Soon he was seated in the barber's chair telling Mr Dyer how he wanted his hair cut. He remarked what a coincidence it was that both barber and client shared the same surname. Then, on a whim, Alan said: "Why don't you call your salon *Cutty Dyer's*?"

The barber gravely replied: "Oh no sir! That would never do. My clientele would fall right off. People round here mind the story of the troll who lurks beneath King's Bridge."

At the mention of the 't' word a sensation like an electric shock passed through Alan's body. He twitched in the chair and Mr Dyer had to move quickly not to cut his ear.

"I'm sorry to alarm you sir. Of course there be no such thing as trolls nowadays. 'Tis an old wives' tale from long ago told to frighten drunken husbands and naughty children. Nobody believes in such things any more," he said.

"Superstition must still exist in these rural areas. Folk memories of past events live on for hundreds of years. The piskies on the moor are probably a memory of the people who lived and farmed up there before the climate changed towards the end of the Dark Ages. Cutty Dyer is probably a folk memory of an unpleasant man who lived near the bridge hundreds of years ago and gained a reputation for violence or something similar," replied Alan who was thinking of how he must cross the little bridge over the rushing water.

"I reckon that trolls, ghosts and suchlike can only harm you if you bother to believe in them. They work on your mind and become real only if you let them," said Mr Dyer as he brushed the last of the hair away from Alan's collar.

"If only I had a choice…" Alan thought to himself.

"There you are sir, that'll be five pounds and ten pence. Thank you very much sir, most generous of you. Come back soon when your hair touches your collar. Good evening sir."

Alan muffled up carefully against the cold that he knew lurked outside the door in the dimly lit passage. The sky had darkened and the wind moaned among the rooftops and chimneys. He walked briskly along Foale's Passage to the wider expanse of North Street. The lamps were coming on shrouded by haloes of fog as the shop lights were switched off. His heart gave a little jump of joy. Of course he could take the long way round to the car park. He would avoid the hump-backed bridge and arrive safely at his car.

What nonsense! Why should he, a grown man with a doctorate and a mortgage, be afraid of something purely imaginary? He would take the short cut, would cross the bridge and conquer his stupid fear of trolls for once and for all. He would laugh at the very thought of a repulsive creature who lurked under the bridge ready to spring out and attack passers by at random.

With a new spring in his step Alan crossed North Street and headed obliquely towards the rising pavement of the little bridge. Through the icy mist he read the sign 'Christopher and Son, Funeral Directors' on the other side of the bridge. He strode up the slight slope and stood by the parapet looking down at the power of the icy waters rushing below him, roaring over a little weir before being swallowed under the road. With his hands in his pockets he stood for a brave moment repeating to himself the words: "There are no trolls."

He recoiled as a heavy hand was brought down hard on his shoulder. He could not help but turn with a terrified gasp to look at the hunched creature standing beside him. A filthy smell reached his chilled nostrils and he gagged. He could not believe the utter foulness of the matted, hairy figure of pure malevolence crouched before him on the crown of the bridge.

"Cutty Dyer…" was all he could say. His weak voice seemed to come from far away inside himself.

"Cutty Dyer that I be, I'm the last thing you'll ever see," croaked the creature, its breath stinking of carrion.

Alan felt himself in the horny grasp of powerful hands and heard the scraping of claws on the surface of the bridge. The creature glared at him with yellow eyes and began to lick his face with a long violet tongue. Tufts of coarse hair brushed against Alan as he vainly struggled to get free of the bent nightmare figure that held him in its iron grip on the icy bridge.

With a desperate shout Alan tried to pull himself free. He would have succeeded if the creature had not hooked a claw through his cheek, tearing the flesh to expose his gritted teeth. With a desperate shriek Alan felt himself lifted up onto the parapet of the bridge. The creature bleated into his ear and released him to the raging flood below. Alan's overstrained heart burst just before his limp body hit the swirling water with a splash.

The troll watched with delight as, with arms and legs bobbing impotently, the body of Alan Dyer was borne swiftly away by the roaring flood. It chuckled as it saw Alan's white face with eyes and torn mouth wide open vanish fluidly round the corner over the weir and under the road. It triumphed in the fact that one more unbeliever had learned the truth about trolls.

Clouds Hill

Even in the month of May the Dorset heath lands retain a drab sadness all of their own. The fresh green leaves on the trees and the trilling of the lark overhead serve only to remind me how quickly the seasons turn and pass.

So it was in a somewhat melancholy frame of mind that I undertook a cycling holiday to explore the southern reaches of Dorset. I was at a loss: I had completed the book I had been writing for the past two years and felt an emptiness like the period of mourning after the death of a close friend. I just had to clear my head. The combination of healthy exercise and fine scenery would lift my spirits. In the meantime I had to cross the somewhat gloomy stretch of heath land north of the Isle of Purbeck.

I could have ridden along the straight main road west of Wareham with the heath forming a low horizon to my right, turning south soon after Wool. But I could not face the thundering traffic and the whining tyres of Army land rovers. So I decided to cycle a little way north west of Wareham to Clouds Hill before turning south across the heath and the tank ranges of Bovington Camp.

In the meantime I could explore the pretty town of Wareham with its earth ramparts and harbour. I booked a room at a comfortable bed and breakfast overlooking the harbour and took a stroll around the town before darkness fell. My attention was taken by a small high-roofed chapel, early mediaeval in origin, which sat at right angles to the main street. Finding the door still open, I stepped inside to find the narrow interior space dominated by a recumbent white marble statue.

The man in Arab robes lay staring at the ceiling, the white orbs of his eyes empty. He wore Arab headdress and long robes with a curved dagger at his waist. I looked closely at the face, both familiar and remote at the same time. The eyes were set close together and had an intensity that denoted great character. The nose was long and aquiline, the mouth straight and firm. The figure exuded presence, a determination that had survived the death of its subject. Two names were carved into the base of the catafalque: The first in small scripted letters was *Eric Kennington,* the second in bold capitals scored deeply into the stone *T.E.Lawrence.*

This then, was a monument to Lawrence of Arabia, scholar, archaeologist, writer, diplomat, soldier, spy; a man riddled with guilt at the betrayal of his allies the Arabs. Here was the man who insisted on spending the latter part of his life in obscurity, shunning publicity and advancement. Here was the man who could not bear to be touched. I took my hand off the marble robe; the man deserved peace even in effigy.

As I turned to leave the darkening chapel I almost felt that I should say a low, respectful greeting. I felt that I was leaving the presence of a great man. Quietly I closed the heavy door of the chapel. The street lights were coming on in the gathering dusk and I walked back to a warm bed and a cup of tea.

Next morning I packed my bicycle and, with a heave of the pedals, was off. I have always been a reluctant cyclist, cursing the hills and taking the valleys for granted. I hate exerting myself and soon found myself quite out of breath as I puffed up the relatively gentle hill out of Wareham. Soon gorse bushes intruded upon the landscape and evidence of heath land became apparent: ditches beside the road, silver birches and a mournful openness. The straight road was levelling out before me. I had a sudden longing for speed and wished momentarily that I was astride a motorcycle rather than a mountain bike.

The spindly trees became more dense and began to meet over my head. I bowled along with the warm breeze in my hair, my spirits rising. The sun flashed through dappled shade. Even the sedge in the ditches had begun to look inviting.

A brown National Trust sign indicated an abrupt left hand turn to Clouds Hill. I noticed with great interest that T.E.Lawrence's cottage was open to visitors and hurried down the lane to turn left at the entrance. I dismounted and pushed my bike up the short gravel drive to a diminutive square brick house beneath a clump of trees. The cottage was painted a stark white and seemed remote, looking inwards rather than out onto the heath that surrounded it on three sides.

I leaned the bike on the trunk of a laurel tree and looked at the immaculate gravel that surrounded the small building. There was nobody to be found, so I walked towards the open front door. Before I had a chance to enter I heard the sound of a large object being pulled across the gravel for a short distance.

Intrigued, I looked carefully round the corner of the cottage to see a man straightening himself up after pulling a large motor bike up onto its stand. My jaw dropped when I saw the bike; it was long and low, compact and solid with not an inch wasted on decoration. Yet it was elegant in a brutal and powerful way. From the basic instruments ranged along the handlebars to the flared exhaust pipes placed one above the other, it expressed raw, unrefined power. It was not a modern machine, the large round headlamp and drab black paint showed that it dated from sometime before the last war. The spare economy of the design took my breath away. Nothing built recently could approach the feral elegance of this powerful beast.

My eye took in everything from the white letters and numbers on the curved front mudguard number plate to the fact that the rear wheel was slightly smaller than the front wheel.

With an effort I turned my attention to the man standing behind the rear wheel. He was somewhat small in stature and frail to be riding such a large and powerful bike. He looked steadily at me as if waiting for me to speak. His hair was a little unkempt after his ride and I saw that it was greying at the temples. He looked straight at me with close set blue eyes that were strangely familiar. Beneath the long nose the jaw was firm.

I wondered if he were the custodian and, if he were, why he was so scruffily dressed in such old fashioned clothes. He wore baggy flannel trousers stained with oil and grease, a white shirt open at the neck and a dark brown V-neck pullover. Most unusually, he wore no socks and worn brown plimsolls on his feet.

He must have been dressed for the same period as the bike, I thought. I saw no helmet as evidence of his recent ride and wondered how he could have got away with such unsafe practice.

As he was still looking directly at me I waved an arm and called to him: "I love the bike, may I have a closer look at it?"

I had obviously said the wrong thing because a look of annoyance crossed the man's face. With a frown he impatiently waved his arm at the road beyond the laurels and, turning on his heel, strode across the gravel to disappear into the interior of the house through the low front door. Sad that I had caused his displeasure, I followed him in order to apologise. There was something familiar about him that I could not, at that moment, explain.

Inside the gloomy entrance hall of the cottage I was politely greeted by a man in a tweed jacket who asked to see my National Trust card. While he was examining it in the shadowy room I asked him if he had seen the man in the brown plimsolls enter the house in front of me.

"No sir," he replied. "You are the first visitor I have seen today. The only person around here to wear brown daps was T.E. himself. They say that his ghost has been seen here. He usually wears long white Arabic robes with a curved dagger at his belt. I have never seen him but Mr Fox, the curator, has seen him on a number of occasions."

I looked curiously around the Spartan interior of the small house. I examined the famous twin sleeping bags, *teum* and *meum*. I noted the aluminium foil insulation on the walls of one of the rooms. I was looking at the faded books in the long bookcase when I heard the roar of a large motorcycle being started. With a crash the kickstart was returned to its place. The motor faltered, then with a muffled explosion, settled into its rhythm as the mixture was adjusted and the choke pushed back in. With a hail of flying gravel, the bike and its rider were off, turning and accelerating hard down the road to Bovington.

I too, had the urge to leave the dark and claustrophobic little house, to be on my way south on the open road. I clattered downstairs and out into the light of a sunny morning. Before I unlocked my bicycle from the trunk of the laurel I bent down to examine the gravel which had been beneath the parked motorcycle. A few drops of fresh oil glistened on the turned flints and the marks of the stand and heavy tyres could be plainly seen.

Once out of the cottage grounds I turned left and headed south over the heath. The road undulated into dips and hollows which made difficult the maintaining of a constant speed. The occasional car passed me by and I could hear the sinister growl of engines and clanking of tracks from the tank ranges that scarred the expanse of heath to my left.

I was freewheeling down into a dip in the dappled shade of roadside trees when I heard the distant roar of a motorcycle. It was some way off but approaching rapidly. I made sure that I was well over on the left hand side of the road. In front of me was another cyclist, a small boy wobbling on what appeared to be a butcher's delivery bicycle. He was almost at the bottom of the dip when he swerved to avoid an old closed black car which suddenly appeared before him in the middle of the road.

The delivery bike swerved onto the right hand side of the road as the driver of the black car angrily shook his fist at the boy. The black car accelerated up out of the dip as the roar of the motorbike steadily increased. The car driver had avoided a collision and was safe; the motorbike rider, now approaching at a tremendous speed was not to be so lucky.

I watched helplessly as the motorbike and rider came rapidly into sight at the top of the dip. The small goggled figure lay along the bike's tank, his arms extended to the handlebars. He must have been doing well over the ton, I thought, as the boy and his heavy bicycle tried to get out of the way.

I could not help but close my eyes as the high screech of rubber on tarmac drilled into my brain. It ended with a rending crash and the splinter of broken glass. Despite myself I opened my eyes to see the heavy motorbike sliding rapidly across the narrow road, ending up in a ditch with its wheels still spinning. Small pieces of trim rattled onto the road surface as the bike came to a rapid halt.

The terrified boy on the bike, still on the wrong side of the road, wobbled rapidly over the brow of the hill and out of sight. I was left alone with the recumbent figure of the motorcyclist sprawled in the middle of the road.

Fortunately the man was unconscious. His injuries must have been terrible. He breathed shallowly and noisily from a nose that had been pulped by the dusty surface of the road. Fresh blood trickled from his ears and his nose. His eyes were shut and his jaw dislocated. My heart beat rapidly as I reached for my mobile phone to call for an ambulance. As I did so I realised that I had, in the last twenty four hours, seen this man twice before. The realisation of this, combined with the shock of witnessing the accident, made my head spin and I must have passed out on the dusty surface of the road.

I came to my senses as a woman cradled my head in her lap. I sat up and looked wildly around. The wrecked motorcycle no longer lay canted in the ditch. The sprawled figure had gone from the middle of the road. A red Ford Ka was parked with an open door beside my recumbent bicycle.

"Thank you," I gasped to the concerned woman and staggered to my feet. I saw no marks on the road, no detached chrome headlamp trim, no blood on the surface of the road. I cast wildly around, doubting for the moment my own sanity.

I walked groggily over to the ditch and bent over. I straightened up with an object in my hand that I waved triumphantly to the bemused woman standing in front of me. There, in my hand, was a worn brown dap, an Army issue plimsoll with the name faintly inked on the faded white inside surface: *T.E.Lawrence.*

Parcere Subjectis

Parcere Subjectis, spare the vanquished, is a strange inscription to put over the main gate of a prison. I certainly thought so when I arrived at H.M.Prison Princetown, handcuffed and heavily guarded, in a black maria in the summer of 1962. I'm an old man now and have gone straight for over forty years, done rather well in the art world if the truth be told. Not bad for an ex forger who was sent down twice.

It was something that happened to me at Dartmoor Prison that changed my attitude and my life. In my case the vanquished was spared in a way that I still find hard to explain.

My name is George Driver and I come from Devonport. When I was a young man I had brains which I was determined not to use. Even though I had a good job as an apprentice draughtsman at the dockyard I got into forging. Blue fivers were my speciality, pretty good they were too. I got caught of course but, after my release, began to specialise in twenties. That was how I came through the granite arch of Dartmoor prison for a five year stretch. At the time one of the guards joked that it should have been a twenty year stretch on account of the forged twenty pound notes.

Five years is a long time on the moor. I missed my trips to Union Street on a Saturday night, walks on the Hoe and Ivor Dewdney pasties. I lived in a damp stone cell and hardly ever got out into the fresh moorland air. Even though I was only seventeen miles from home I lived in a different world. My fingers were sore from sewing mailbags and I can't say that I liked the company of murderers, rapists and thieves very much. Being the smart arse that I was, I was determined to escape and find my way home where I could hide out until I could take ship for some part of the world where I could begin a new life.

Princetown is a miserable place, just a village to serve the prison. It is cold and wet for most of the time. The westerlies bring in curtains of rain that shroud the moor for days on end. The fog is down for a lot of the time, a cold damp mist that muffles sound and takes away all sense of scale and distance. In the winter we have a penetrating frost for weeks and a wind that flays a man alive. All these weather conditions are ideal for escape.

Do you remember the winter of '62? It was by far the worst of the century. Snow blanketed the moor for months, drifting in places over ten feet high. Water pipes remained frozen for weeks on end. Some of the warders' houses lost electricity and water. We were reasonably alright in the prison; the generators ran night and day to keep us warm and fed. On clear days the sun shone sparkling off the snowfield that surrounded the prison blocks. Sometimes we could hear the clatter of the helicopters dropping hay to the ponies and sheep.

After Christmas there was no let up. The wind continued to blow and the snow to fall. I could tell that a lot of the warders were getting fed up and demoralised by the conditions that they had to endure. Security was becoming lax and opportunities for escape more frequent.

January dragged its frozen days into February with no sign of a break or thaw. I was on an outside work party fetching the cows into the prison dairy to be milked in the morning and taking them back out to their stalls in the farm.

On a particularly nasty day Mr Pascoe, the warder in charge of the work detail, showed every sign of coming down with the 'flu. He was morose and irritable and just wanted to stay in the warm with the cows as they were being milked. Thirty cows can generate a lot of heat between them. Outside the wind moaned dismally and black ice coated the concrete surface of the yard in ripples.

"Driver, do I really need to come across the yard with you to fetch the next batch of cows?" he muttered between clenched teeth.

"Not really Sir," I replied knowing that my opportunity had come at last.

As the newly milked cows clattered and slid their way out of the shed into the yard I saw that the fog was blotting out every familiar feature. I slapped the last bony rump as it left the relative warmth of the shippon.

"You stay here Sir. You can rely on me to bring in the last dozen cows from across the yard. I won't let you down Sir," I said trying to keep my voice low and even. "One thing though. It's freezing out there, so can I borrow your coat for a couple of minutes?"

Pascoe looked at me with rheumy eyes. His nose ran and his face was ghastly pale. He had probably come to work this morning just to get away from his damp freezing house. I was doing him a favour, really. Soon he would not have to endure these harsh conditions of employment any more. He would probably lose his pension, but so what? I would gain my freedom: I would win and he would lose.

"Alright lad, here you go. But I want it back the minute you bring those cows in here. It's bloody cold in here with the door open."

I walked out into the yard wrapped in the warder's dark blue greatcoat. I couldn't believe my luck. My nailed boots slid on a frozen cowpat as I looked over to the hazy outline of the other side of the yard. I knew the layout by heart so all I had to do was cross the frozen concrete and open the door to the cowshed. Then I climbed over the gate, up a granite wall, round some sheds and out onto the open moor. Nobody heard or saw me in the dreary frozen fog that lay like a shroud above the thousand foot contour.

Once away from the yard I had to contend with the thick snow whose frozen crust I broke every time I took a step. It was most unlikely that I would meet anyone, but the blue battledress trousers and dark blue greatcoat would make most people think that I was a warder on patrol. Only the most observant would notice that I was not wearing a peaked cap.

The lack of any kind of hat was a problem. I was beginning to feel very cold. After half an hour I had lost most of the feeling in my hands and feet and my harsh prison haircut exposed my ears to the blast of the east wind. I trudged doggedly on, the bottoms of my trousers were icing up and beginning to drag at my hips. It was hard to walk enclosed in a frozen world of my own with only the harsh sound of my breathing and the muffled crunch of frozen snow under my worn boots.

At last I reached the top of the long hill and walked straight into one of the cables that held up the radio mast on North Hessary Tor. I was flung back onto the hard snow with a bloody nose but at least I knew where I was. I would head generally downhill towards Burrator Reservoir and Dousland, coming off the Moor near Yelverton if all went well. After that I was almost home and dry.

But I had not considered the harshness of the weather. Visibility was practically zero. I walked in a frozen twilight even though it was not yet midday. The worst thing was the cold which penetrated like a dead hand, robbing me of the wish to continue. I realised that I was ravenously hungry and unfit after almost a year's incarceration. Yet I struggled on, now sliding downhill, now labouring uphill fighting for breath, with red dots swarming in front of my eyes.

I had no idea where I was. I repeatedly fell down on the hard crusty ground. After a particularly hard fall I lay winded on the icy moor. It took all my willpower to pull myself up onto my feet. As I stood weak and swaying I heard a man's voice, muffled and close, from just a few feet away.

"Come on Driver. Get a move on Carlin. Do you want to die like sparrows on this godforsaken moor?"

The voices seemed to come from all around me, magnified and made hollow by the fog. With a

158

start I recognised my own name. Could they have sent out a search party for me already?

"I can go no further Corporal Penton, I've no strength left." This voice spoke in an Irish brogue and whined in desperation.

Corporal? I thought. Had they sent out the Army to save me? I didn't care now for freedom, I just wanted to get away from the nightmare of the trackless wastes that I thought I knew so well.

"March, you malingering bastards. Follow me unless you wish to die out here and have them find your bleached bones in the spring." The words came closer now. They seemed to be behind me now even though I had seen no figures pass. I could have lain down on the hard snow and closed my eyes for ever.

Wearily I turned round and followed the voice up the hill I had just laboriously come down. I could just make out two sets of indistinct tracks made by nailed boots. Didn't the Army use Dunlop Moulded Soles these days? I remembered my days of national service. I couldn't see the men in front of me but was determined to try to keep up with them so I would not have to be alone. My breath seared my chest and I felt weak and dizzy. If they could keep going then so could I.

I trudged weakly on after the voices. After a while they stopped and the fog cleared a little. In front of me I could just make out the indistinct shape of a tall man on his own. I wondered what had happened to the two privates. By now I didn't really care. My whole face hurt and I felt far removed from warmth and reality. So long as one man led the way for me I didn't care if he were Harold Macmillan.

I floundered through drifts on the slopes of North Hessary Tor. The snow was falling once again in dense whirling sheets, obscuring even the cables that supported the radio mast. I only had the Corporal to guide me, a wavering shape that seemed to drift a few yards in front of me.

At the end of my resources I stopped and sank down in the fresh snow, not giving a monkey's whether I lived or died. The indistinct figure of the Corporal loomed over me. He wore a long grey coat and had buttoned leggings up to the knees of his black serge trousers. Like me he was hatless. I noticed the shiny brass number sevens on the raised collar of his coat. His voice seemed to reach my ears from all around me.

"Driver, listen to me! We are at Soldier's Pond. I may go no further."

He peered intently at me. I saw the ice clinging to his long sideboards. He was young and very pale. He raised an arm and pointed into the gloom. I blinked and looked up at the empty space that he had just occupied. I rose heavily to my feet and stumbled the two hundred yards to the road that led to the Prison

Officers' Club, ready to give myself up to the nearest screw.

Was I scared? Not at the time, only later on. With what little intelligence I had remaining I made my painful way through the whirling snowflakes back to the Prison Dairy. I wondered if Pascoe was still there, if he was still on duty.

Half frozen I stumbled into the warmth of the shippon. Pascoe lay asleep on the damp straw breathing heavily through his nose. I shook him awake.

"Here's you coat Sir. I'm back." Someone had milked the last twelve cows and let them out to make their way back to their shed. I never found out who had done that. Pascoe was delirious with a high temperature and I helped him back to the main part of the prison. He kept his job and his pension and I received a commendation for helping him. I became a model prisoner and was released early, never to re-offend.

Why three unfortunate soldiers who had died in snowdrifts one hundred and ten years ago came back to save my life I'll never know. The effect it had on me was to make me turn myself around and become a person who thought of more than just myself.

An Adventure

On a brilliant late June morning in 1916 Anne Moberly put down her paper in the breakfast room of The Royal Lion Hotel, peered over the top of her round spectacles and announced to her friend Eleanor Jordain: "Today we shall walk to the Undercliff."

Not at all put off by her older companion's slightly imperious tone Miss Jordain replied: "Certainly, Annie. We shall order picnics from the kitchen and be off before ten."

The two maiden ladies had arrived the day before in Lyme Regis for a week's holiday from the academic rigors of Oxford. Miss Jordain had recently succeeded Miss Moberly as Principal of St Hugh's College, a small and highly respected institution of higher learning for girls. Miss Moberly agreed to celebrate her active retirement by sharing a week by the sea in Dorset with her oldest and best friend. They had taken two rooms at the front of the venerable bow fronted hotel with its view of the Channel and the tumbled hills of west Dorset.

As Anne carefully placed the folded paper on the breakfast table Eleanor glanced once again at the headline: **Bombardment on the Somme begins. The Big Push is on.** She gathered up her book and sketchbook and went to her room to change into clothes suitable for a day's walking. She had a slight headache but thought that it would go when the two ladies set off for their walk.

It was a truly sparkling day. The sun shone from an azure sky in which the only clouds were lines of fluffy towers miles out over the Channel. A lazy offshore breeze caused a slight oily swell on the placid surface of the sea. The occasional wink of light from a breaking billow broke the monotony of the water.

Anne and Eleanor stood in front of the hotel facing the curve of the bay. The noises of the town rose around them, the roll of milk churns and barrels, the clatter of horses' hooves on the cobbles, the hoarse cries of fishermen. The ladies wore their straw sun hats and carried their sketch books, pencils and picnics in haversacks. Eleanor thought of the thousands of soldiers waiting in their trenches in France to begin the attack that would push back the armies of the Kaiser and secure a great victory for the Allies.

The sounds of the town began to recede as the ladies strode along the front towards the Cobb, the ancient stone harbour wall that curved out into the Channel like a bent finger beckoning boats to a safe haven. Behind them Golden Cap reared its truncated pyramid above the treacherous and shaley cliffs of the Dorset coast.

Eleanor pushed her wire glasses back onto the bridge of her nose and tucked a wayward strand of greying hair into her straw hat. Her head throbbed with a rhythmical pressure that was increasingly intrusive. She could feel a faint series of percussions but hear nothing that could have caused it. A slight sweat broke on her forehead as she walked gamely on.

Soon all that could be heard were the plaintive cries of gulls and the trilling of a solitary lark far overhead. The throbbing percussions persisted and Eleanor turned to Anne and said: "I feel a little unwell this morning. No doubt I am still tired from the journey. Do you mind if I sit down for a moment on the harbour wall?"

"Of course I don't mind, Eleanor. We are on holiday you know," Anne replied.

"Can't you hear the explosions, or rather feel them?" asked Eleanor as she sat on the rough harbour wall.

"No, I really can hear nothing of the sort. The bombardment on the Somme is over two hundred miles away and no sound can carry that far. You must be thinking of your nephew Charles who must be over there in the thick of it. We have to trust to God to keep him safe."

"You're right of course dear Annie. Charles is on my mind and will be until he is home safe and sound. They say that the life of a Second Lieutenant at the front is hard and short. Indeed it is in the hands of God and to worry is a negation of our faith."

Eleanor felt relieved and knew that she could continue with the walk. She stood resolutely up and gathered her things about her. The distant booming continued to assail her ears but she determined to ignore it.

"Just a touch of nerves, Annie. No doubt the walk will do us both good and help us to put our cares on one side for a while."

The two friends walked over a shingle bank towards the lowering cliffs beneath which they would find the path which led to Seaton. The land soon began to slope towards the tumbled grandeur of the cliffs. They strode up a flowery meadow to a rough stone wall where a sign proclaimed **County Gate.**

"We are about to leave Dorset for Devon," said Anne.

"I shall stay here in this field and sketch the cliffs above us. The quality of the light is just so and I still feel a little tired. You go on and explore the Undercliff and I'll stay here to wait for you in the next county," replied Eleanor.

"A good idea," said the older woman. "I'll walk along the path and look at the flora and fauna. I'll be no more than two hours and I'll meet you here."

Anne turned and, with a little wave to her younger friend, walked off to the end of the rough path. Soon Eleanor saw her stocky form disappear round a clump of trees. She was a little relieved to be alone. She needed to rest and to think.

Her nephew Charles had just come down from Cambridge with a First in Theology. If he survived the war he was destined for the church. He was such a nice young man, so amusing and cultured. It seemed wrong that he was out in France living in squalor and constant danger, associating with men who were rough and even depraved. A good preparation for a curacy in a town parish she supposed. May God keep him safe and preserve him.

The throbbing percussions had settled down to a regular rhythm in Eleanor's head. They were indisputably real and Eleanor looked far out to sea in the direction from which they seemed to come. She was surprised to see that the line of towering white clouds had turned dark and threatening. They were a long way off and did not seem to be moving at all. The sun still shone with its reassuring warmth; just one corner of the fair blue sky had turned a deep pulsating purple shot through with red flashes which corresponded to the thudding in Eleanor's tired brain.

With an effort of will she turned away and looked hard at the cliffs towering above the path her friend had taken. Lofty brows of pale stone rose from a chaos of undergrowth, clumps of wild trees, acres of vines and brambles and the occasional sloping small field. The cliffs seemed to be suspended above the tumbled land below in a temporary compromise that might last for a few minutes of for centuries. She saw her friend, now a stout dot, making her way across a clearing half a mile away. She was a little reassured by the sight. Why did she feel that her physical nearness to a person would ensure their safety? A ridiculous notion and, once again, a negation of her Christian faith.

Eleanor turned to her book and began to sketch. She became totally absorbed in capturing the difficult details of the scene in front of her. She did not notice that the livid line of clouds over the Channel had reverted to its former peaceful towering whiteness and held no further menace for Eleanor or anyone else on the Dorset coast.

She was having difficulty reproducing the angles of the sloping cliff scenery, its intersecting planes and seamed shaded areas. She looked away from her smudged paper to see a tall ash tree on the lofty cliff's immediate edge wave frantically back and forth before crashing among a shower of large stones into a gully far out of sight. As she sprang up in a panic she saw a whole section of cliff, about half a mile long, slowly detach itself from the edge of the land and begin a disintegrating slide into the sea far below. Huge boulders fell and bounced high into the air as thousands of tons of cliff crashed towards the quiet sea below.

Soon the noise of the landslip reached Eleanor's frantic ears. It was a rending of shattered trees, a crash of falling rocks and an immense sliding and splashing of tortured land. She could not believe that the scene she had tried to record in her sketch book over the last hour had changed for ever, taking houses, farms and livestock and sweeping them, mangling them and drowning them in the angry sea.

What about Annie, her dear old friend? Had she been smashed, buried beyond all help beneath ruptured earth and shattered rock? Please God grant that it was not so. With that agonising thought Eleanor collapsed in a faint on the soft turf of the field.

Time had elapsed when she struggled back to a miserable consciousness. She sat up with a terrible sense of loss but with no more of the sensation of heavy guns bursting in her head. Walking placidly towards her was a young man in the khaki uniform of an army officer.

On his shoulder were the three pips of a captain. It was Charles, but a slightly older Charles. On the breast of his filthy tunic was the ribbon of the

Military Cross. His right arm was held in a grubby sling and his whipcord breeches were torn and spattered with mud.

"Aunt Eleanor, it's me. Don't look so worried, in a few days it will all be over. At eleven o'clock on November the eleventh the armistice will be signed. By then I'll be almost home. My arm is mending nicely but will keep me out of action until it is all over. May God be praised for sparing my life against all odds," he said. His voice was tired but vibrant. He had dark circles under his eyes and his face was lined but he was alive and triumphantly so.

"I must go now. I have the men to look after before I am sent home. I will see you soon. Goodbye Aunt Eleanor."

As he faded from view Eleanor saw a stouter figure stumping out of the far clump of trees from the ravished landscape beyond. Anne approached her friend with a look of concern on her face.

"What's the matter, Eleanor dear? I've only been gone two hours and I find you pale and anxious. This will not do you know," she said.

"He will be alright. I know for sure he will. He will survive the war and become a vicar. But how did you get through the landslip? How did you survive? I saw the cliff come crashing down. Where were you?"

"The landslip happened a long time ago, in 1839 to be precise. I saw a print of it in the window of an antique shop in London the other day. You could not have seen it happen today. Let me see your drawing. Extraordinary! How could you have the imagination to draw the cliffs as they were before they crashed into the sea all those years ago...?"

Mrs Carey-Carew

"So you're the new gardener. Welcome. I hope we'll manage to keep you longer than all the others. None stayed for long although the work isn't too demanding. I'm getting on and suffer increasingly from rheumatism so most of the work is care and maintenance."

Miss Carey-Carew stood welcomingly in the front doorway of her ancient hilltop house. She beckoned Henry in and sat him down in the cluttered kitchen. She was a plump, jolly woman with straggling grey hair tied in a bun.

She continued: "The house has been in the family for generations. Parts of it go back to Tudor times."

It was indeed a remarkable house, built on a terrace above a deep valley and surrounded by dense woods. Henry had found it difficult to reach and had been relieved to find it suddenly in front of him when he eventually rounded the last bend in the steep narrow drive. The front of the house overlooked sloping mossy lawns while one side rose above a terrace from which could be seen distant views of woods and fields. Tall trees seemed to compete for light and air as they reached above the steep roofs and irregular chimneys of the house.

Henry thought that the terraced side of the house had a rather Mediterranean look. With its flat wall painted terra cotta and blue shutters beside the windows, the house could have overlooked a mountainous shore with the sea sparkling in the distance. It could even overlook a Swiss lake, like the Villa Deodato, where such a lot happened to those writers with romantic imaginations during a wet fortnight's holiday nearly two hundred years ago.

"…and I would like you to clear out the borders and get rid of the ground elder as well as the blasted willowherb. Dead head all those marguerites and pull up the small ash trees which have proliferated these last couple of years. Is all that quite clear?"

"Certainly, Miss Carey-Carew."

Henry was not just a gardener. He was completing his doctoral thesis on The Romantic poets' view of nineteenth century scientific progress. This made him at times a rather distant and dreamy individual. He knew his gardens however and was a thorough and a tireless worker when his mind was on the matter in hand.

"You may call me Kitty, you know. I don't think that you are a young man to take advantage."

Henry saw a decided twinkle in Miss Carey-Carew's faded blue eyes. He also noticed an absent look which corresponded to his musings about the Villa Deodato.

He set to work with a will. The sky cleared and the tufted pine trees set against the clear blue sky increased Henry's musings. He pulled at thistles and tugged at brambles and filled his sack with weeds. He was quite ready to stop and gratefully accept the cup of tea that Kitty brought out to him on the lawn. She motioned him into a rusty chair and fixed him with her determined blue eyes.

"I have lived here all my life. I never married, you know. It was probably the shock of my father's disappearance when I was eighteen. My mother said that he had left her to go off to live in the south of France. We never heard from him again.

He was a good man but he never fulfilled my mother's expectations of him. He never became particularly wealthy. He never made an effort to push himself forward.

I never had any brothers or sisters, you know. A pity, because my father was a wonderful father. I think my mother disapproved of the attention he gave me. She was jealous and so when he suddenly left it was a relief to her. For a while she was a new woman, all sparkle and joy. But after a while depression set in and she faded away. She was dead before I was twenty-five.

I have always been of a solitary nature, so I was content to stay here and let time pass comfortably. I have a lot of my father in me, you see."

"Yes," thought Henry; "her father and I have a lot in common; a quiet life with time for thought and contemplation. I wonder what became of him."

"If I were to travel to Nice or Menton I might find my father's grave in some French hillside cemetery. But what would that prove? Only that he is dead; he could no longer be living today."

"The answer could be nearer to home than we think," said Henry suddenly. He wondered why he had said those words. He had no idea how to solve the mystery of an obscure disappearance that happened over fifty years ago.

"He never had any financial worries. He was as honest as the day is long. Sometimes people do things that are completely at odds with their normal way of acting."

Henry went back to work refreshed but more than a little puzzled. Why should this sad old story affect him so much? As he bent to his digging of the tangled borders he had a distinct feeling that he would in some way find out what really happened to Mr Bertram Carey-Carew.

After lunch the sky clouded over and a thundery glaucous light suffused the garden. Insect swarmed round Henry's head as he sweated at his work. A hush descended on the grounds of the old house. A slanting sun glanced off the dark windows of the house in needles of light that caused Henry to squint against the glare.

A figure moved noiselessly across the lawn towards him. Kitty laid a gnarled hand on Henry's shoulder.

"Tomorrow, if it doesn't rain, I should like you to work on the old patio. There is such a lovely view from there, you know. We cannot use it at the moment because part of it has subsided. Could you rebuild the walls and set the paving straight for me? Then we could have our tea on it in the mornings and afternoons and admire the prospect of the wooded hills."

"Certainly Kitty. That is a job I would really enjoy. I love restoring old things and giving them a new lease of life."

Next day Henry arrived for work with a song in his heart. He had his masonry hammer and excavation tools ready for the task ahead. It was obvious that the raised seating area at the edge of the terrace had collapsed with the passing years. All the walls would have to be carefully dismantled and rebuilt. The paving slabs would have to be taken up, numbered and laid on one side while several tons of hardcore and sand would be used to fill the cavity. Then the slabs would be carefully put back and the stone urns and lead cherubs cleaned and secured in their original positions.

The whole project would take most of a week's work; a far cry from pulling up dandelions and clipping holly bushes. At last a job with real permanence, thought Henry.

He looked up from his calculations to see a tall thin woman in black clothes standing by the ruined patio. He was surprised to see a family resemblance; the woman was a younger, slimmer version of Kitty. But there the likeness ended.

The standing woman had none of Kitty's warmth. Her eyes were of an icy blue. She stared piercingly at Henry, her thin lips pursed. She did not move, but fixed Henry with a hostile, malevolent stare that held no warmth of feeling. In her left hand she held a long pair of scissors with which she had obviously been deadheading roses.

Henry realised with a shock that there were no roses left to deadhead. He had completed that job yesterday with his usual thoroughness. The woman slowly raised her left arm in a gesture of menace. Then she turned and walked slowly away into the shrubs behind her. Henry was shaken by the malevolence shown by the woman. He wondered if Kitty had a younger cousin who sometimes visited the house and who had grown attached to the garden as it was.

He turned back to the task in hand. First of all he had to remove the heavy stone slabs from the top of the patio. This took several hours because the slabs were so heavy that it took all of Henry's strength to move and stack them. When the end of the day came Henry forgot to ask who the women with the scissors had been.

Next day dawned hot and thundery. Henry was determined to consolidate the area under the slabs and began to excavate the hollow area in the middle of the patio. As he dug he felt a presence behind him. Knowing what he would see he reluctantly straightened up and turned to see the thin woman in the black dress standing a few feet in front of him.

If anything her expression was even more menacing than before. The blue eyes held an intensity that was fuelled by pure hate. It was if the woman were silently commanding Henry to stop digging. But Henry was determined to continue and knew that the woman before him was not real, was powerless to stop him from completing his task.

"Go away!" he shouted at the drawn white face. "You're not real, you cannot stop me!"

Another voice came to him from across the lawn.

"What's the matter Henry?" Kitty hurried towards him with an anxious look on her face.

"So you've seen her too. I was afraid that this might happen. She hasn't been back for months but any change in the garden seems to attract her. I'm so very sorry, I should have warned you. But then you wouldn't have stopped to work here."

"Who is the woman? I must know if I am to continue here. At least you owe me that, Kitty."

"It is the unhappy wraith of my mother who died here long ago. She seems unable to leave us now. We must continue with the work; it is important not to let her influence what we are doing. The dead must have no bearing on the living, I fully believe that."

Reassured by Kitty's determined presence Henry bent down once again to his excavations. He relaxed a little as he shovelled loose sand out of the hole in order to reach the foundations. He shovelled the sand and earth into a neat pile beside the wall of the patio. As he did so he began to notice a faint musty smell seeping up from the hole.

Feeling the cold blue eyes boring into him as he worked, Henry continued his digging. He could not decide which was worse, the looming visible presence of the woman or her invisible malevolent stare.

Three feet into the hole Henry felt something hard under the blade of his shovel. He brushed aside the dry earth to expose two long stick-like bones.

Because he had spent several summers on archaeological digs Henry was not overtly alarmed, merely curious. With a sinking sense of inevitability he brushed the soil away with his hand. The pelvic bones that came into view were obviously human. The curve of a spine and a collapsed cluster of ribs confirmed the inevitable.

Then Henry saw something that brought him to his feet with a start. Protruding through the sternum were the rusted handles of a long pair of scissors. Henry bent down with a real sense of fear, feeling the evil presence so close to him that he expected momentarily to feel a cold hand laid on his shoulder. With a tremendous effort of will he brushed the dark sandy soil from the face of the skull. The teeth gleamed dully and the eye sockets were full of earth. A little hair still adhered to the domed brow.

As Henry completed his exposure of the bones he deduced that he was looking at the skeleton of a man in early middle age. The forbidding atmosphere of dread and menace had turned to intense sorrow. Henry straightened his tired back and leaned slightly back. He felt a light blow on his arm and heard a long howl of pure anguish which seemed to come not from one spot in the garden but from all around him. Then all was quiet and peaceful at long last.

"Henry, are you alright? That was my mother's voice. I think she has left us now."

Kitty walked rapidly over to the hole in the middle of the patio. Henry heard her deep intake of breath as she saw her father for the first time in over fifty years.

It wasn't William…

They drove for miles between high hedges, round sharp corners, up and down steep hills until, at last, they reached Hemsworthy House buried deep in the South Hams. As they turned into the short drive they were relieved to see Mr Lethbridge of Lethbridge, Legrand and Pearce, estate agents of Kingsbridge, standing on the lawn in front of the house.

Tom switched off the motor and set foot on the gravel. Catherine opened her door and stood up to face the house.

"It's beautiful," she said. "I love the proportions of the windows. It has a good feel. I like this one."

Tom sighed inwardly. How many times had he heard similar sentiments from his wife to find later reservations creep in like dark clouds obscuring the sun? He disliked most houses on first impression, needing to be won over. This house was different however.

It sat foursquare in about an acre of gently sloping garden. The rough stone finish of the walls failed to detract from the classic Georgian proportions of regular well-placed windows which diminished in size as they reached the third floor. On the south face of the house was a pillared portico in white-painted wood behind which was the imposing front door. The house sat well under a solid roof of Delabole slate which looked to be in good order. Tom liked the remote and self-contained feeling of the house.

"...built in 1789 for a local family who were prominent in the shipping trade," said Mr Lethbridge. "It changed hands only once in over two hundred years after a fire which resulted in a partial rebuilding. Let me show you the inside."

He pulled a large iron key from the pocket of his Barbour and ushered the couple up the steps onto the pillared porch. Catherine felt the warm sun on her back as she turned to follow the two men into the long hallway. An owl hooted repeatedly from the densely wooded valley below the house.

The rooms were a delight, well proportioned and cosy with Adam fireplaces and dark wallpaper. The kitchen, although large, was warm and snug with an enormous Aga and a good view of the walled garden.

Tom was delighted by the cellars and outbuildings which he knew he and Catherine could make very good use of.

They had moved reluctantly from Devon to London to paint and work in a new gallery. Their work sold so well that soon they owned the gallery and bought quite a large house in Chiswick. But they missed the Westcountry and were principled enough not to buy a second home to visit at weekends and on high days and holidays. One day they looked at each other and said "enough". So they were spending their summer holiday looking at houses while capable employees ran the gallery.

The bedrooms and bathrooms delighted the couple and quite won them over. Steep stairs led to the former servants' quarters, snug rooms with ceilings that sloped under the roof.

"These are the rooms with the best views," said Catherine. Both she and Tom were taken with the corner room which had a feeling remote from the rest of the house. It had a view directly down into the valley where a river twinkled below the thick overhanging trees.

Despite the few Victorian changes which must have resulted from the fire, the whole house had an authentically Georgian feel that appealed greatly to both Tom and Catherine. After a thorough tour of house and grounds Tom and Catherine sat down with

Mr Lethbridge in the dusty and sparsely furnished dining room.

"During the Napoleonic Wars the house was used to house paroled French officers; in fact an ancestor of our Mr Legrand spent three years here," concluded Mr Lethbridge.

Tom raised his eyes. "Why is the asking price for this magnificent house so relatively modest?" he asked.

Mr Lethbridge considered his reply carefully. "It is said that the house has a ghost," he said at last. "Perfectly harmless; a servant girl I believe. Of course I've never seen or felt anything on my numerous visits here so I can give the story no credence. It has put a lot of people off, however. It's the idea that folk don't like of sharing their home, but, frankly I don't believe a word of it myself."

The visit drew to a satisfactory close and, within a few weeks, Tom and Catherine packed up their affairs in London and moved into Hemsworthy House. They certainly did not believe in ghosts but still felt that they had been somehow chosen to live there.

Towards the close of a brilliant autumn day Catherine discovered the pond in a little courtyard under a willow tree. Why she had not seen it before puzzled her. It was a small clear pond, usually in shade for most of the day.

She knelt down to look into the clear water. As she wondered how deep the pond was she was aware of someone watching her. She looked up quickly, expecting to see Tom peering round a corner at her. There was nobody there and, with an exasperated sigh, Catherine looked back into the quiet depths of the pool.

The surface of the water shimmered and Catherine clearly saw the reflection of a female figure in a long dark dress standing beside her. She looked up again to see no-one there. When she looked back at the water's surface she saw the woman once again, young and pale with her hands clasped in front of her dark dress. Her eyes were large and imploring, wisps of fair hair straggled from her cap.

Catherine was not at all afraid. "Can I help you my dear?" she murmured.

A sibilant voice seemed to whisper in her ear: "I am Sarah. I can never leave here to be happy. A terrible thing has happened…" The slight voice faded away leaving Catherine confused and close to tears.

Later that evening she broached the subject to Tom as they sat in the dusky kitchen enjoying the warmth of the Aga.

"Tom, I think I saw the ghost today. I think she was a servant girl from Cornwall. She was trying to tell me something and wasn't at all frightening. We must try to help her."

Tom nodded his head. "I have been catching glimpses of someone in a long dark dress from the corner of my eye for a couple of days now. I think we must do some research into the history of this house. I feel very sorry for this girl and want to know more."

Catherine gave him a hug. "I feel somehow responsible for Sarah. She came along with the house and is asking us for some sort of resolution."

Next day the couple took time off from directing the business of the London gallery and drove along the winding lane to Kingsbridge. They loved the small town with its bulbous Town Hall clock and its views of hills and estuary. They soon found the offices of the *Kingsbridge Chronicle* in a tall Georgian house at the top of the High Street.

After a couple of hours of examining microfiches of newspaper articles they found what they had been looking for:

Kingsbridge Chronicle   September 17th 1874:

Fire at Hemsworthy House: Tragic Death of Servant. Extensive Damage to Fabric and Structure of House.

Last night the Nicholls family suffered a double tragedy as their mansion burned out of control. Their maid servant, Sarah Roscruge, aged 19, of Liskeard, perished in the inferno. Her charred remains were found soon after the fire had finally been brought under control by the Kingsbridge Fire Company in the early hours of this morning.

The blazing inferno appeared to start in the butler's pantry and soon spread up the main staircase to rapidly consume the greater part of the servants' quarters on the third floor. The damage is considered so extensive that the family will be forced to find alternative accommodation while they decide whether they will repair the damage and continue to occupy the tragic house.

Mr Treleaven, our senior correspondent, reports that flames thirty feet high could be seen at the height of the fire shooting from the roof accompanied by extensive showers of sparks and the most horrid crackling of dry combustible materials.

He wonders what the future hold for Mr and Mrs Nicholls whose shipping business has recently been beset by loss and tragedy after the recent foundering at sea, with the loss of all hands, of the barque Mary Hoskins.

Kingsbridge Chronicle   September 20th 1874:

Hemsworthy Fire Tragedy: Butler Found and Arrested.

Yesterday a new series of events cast light on the tragic mystery of the devastating fire at Hemsworthy House.   Local   constables   apprehended   William

Hutchings, formerly the butler at the above establishment. Mr Hutchings was unable to be found after the tragic blaze in which a servant unfortunately lost her life. The constables wished to question him as to how the fire originated. It appears to have started in the butler's pantry before rapidly spreading to other parts of the house.

Mr Hutchings was found concealed in Mr Rogers' barn and had to be brought out by force. He will appear before the Magistrate, Mr Pope, on Thursday next, in the meanwhile being confined under restraints in the Town Hall cells.

"Well!" said Catherine, her eyes wide with surprise. "That's quite enough for one day. We can come back when we learn more from Sarah."

Indeed Sarah did not delay in visiting the couple in the early hours of the morning when both Tom and Catherine awoke simultaneously from a deep sleep. She stood at the foot of the bed, surrounded by a luminous glow, wringing her hands. Catherine sat up at once with beating heart and said quietly: "What is it Sarah?"

The wraith replied: "It wasn't William. Believe me ma'am, it never was William." Then, exhausted by her utterance, she began to gradually fade leaving the room in thick darkness.

Next morning Tom and Catherine drove straight back to Kingsbridge through morning mist and heaps of fallen leaves. Mrs Tucker at the office of the *Kingbridge Chronicle* greeting the couple with a rising excitement in her voice:

"I knew you would be back. I have done a little more research into the Hemsworthy fire and I must show you what I have found…"

She placed a large photocopied article on the cluttered desk in front of them.

Kingbridge Chronicle   September 24th 1874:

Death of butler implicated in the fire at Hemsworthy House:

Last evening the body of William Hutchings was found in his cell at the Kingsbridge Town Hall. It was evident from the quantity of blood on the body and from the deep wound in his throat that he had taken his own life, thus escaping the undoubted consequences of his guilty act in setting the fire at Hemsworthy House which claimed the life of one of the maidservants. No knife or razor was found either in the cell or in the vicinity of the tragedy.

Mr and Mrs Nicholls, the devastated owners of the mansion, were absent and so unavailable to comment on the dire events which unfolded in the cells. They have apparently decided to remove to London, being unable to face a return to the scene of the tragedy. Their agent, Mr Sykes of Plymouth, declared that the remains of the house would be put on the market at the earliest possible convenience.

Mr Hutchings, a man with a previously unsullied character, was due to appear before the magistrate, Mr Pope, a cousin of Mr and Mrs Nicholls, on the morrow.

"I don't think we've seen the last of Sarah…" said Tom thoughtfully. Mrs Tucker gave him a questioning look.

"…figuratively speaking, of course."

That evening the house took on a brooding air as if waiting for something to happen. The solitary owl hooted continuously from the wooded valley and gnats danced in clouds over the darkening lawn. All was hushed and unnaturally quiet. As the sun sank below the hill and the amber moon rose, Tom and Catherine sat in the warm kitchen with the lights out waiting for Sarah to confirm their suspicions about and event that had happened over a hundred and thirty years ago and still cast its long shadow on the house and its inhabitants both living and dead.

They must have dozed because the sharp smell of smoke took them both by surprise. Tom climbed the stairs smelling more acutely the acrid smoke. He turned to Catherine who resolutely followed him with a heavy torch in her hand.

"The fire seems to be coming from the attic. Hurry, we must find it," whispered Tom not quite believing that there really was a fire.

As they came to the top step of the attic staircase they saw a fiery glow spreading from the corner room. Outlined clearly by the pulsing flames were two dark figures standing hand in hand on the landing. They recognised the familiar figure of Sarah looking beseechingly at them. Her companion was a tall young man in the dark formal clothes of a butler. Slowly and deliberately he raised his arm and pointed to the glowing doorway of the corner room.

"It's alright Sarah," called Catherine. "We're going in. Thank you. May you both now rest in peace."

A fleeting look of great relief crossed Sarah's face and she turned to William before they were both gone, like the snuffing out of a candle. Tom and Catherine rushed into the corner room where the smell of smoke had begun to fade leaving a glowing orb pulsating halfway up the wall by the fireplace. Tom shakily reached over and marked the spot with a pencil and the couple left the room hand in hand with only the beam of the torch to show them the way.

Next morning, after a restless and disturbed night's sleep, Tom and Catherine climbed the steep attic stairs with a lump hammer and cold chisel. It was clear that a rough place in the plaster marked the spot shown to them by the orb. A few blows of the hammer and rotten plaster crumbled out of a hidden niche in the wall.

"There's a box in there," said Catherine with a catch in her voice. "And I'm pretty sure I know what it contains."

The gold wedding ring proved her right. The words *Sarah* and *William* roughly engraved on the inside of the band laid bare the whole tragic story.

"…so Sarah Roscruge and William Hutchings were secretly married. They had to keep it secret for fear of Sarah losing her position in service and being sent away far from her husband. The gentry took a very dim view of their servants marrying or conducting any sort of romantic relationship in those days.

The Nicholls were in desperate financial straits. The loss of their barque the *Mary Hoskins* gave them the idea to set fire to their house and claim the insurance money. Their status as gentry gave them a cast iron alibi in those days. They would blame the whole thing on the butler William Hutchings who would not dare contradict them because he was in his wife's bedroom when the fire was set. But they had not foreseen the tragic death of Sarah in the scheme of things.

William had to be silenced and it was possible that Mr Pope the magistrate and cousin of Mr Nicholls had him murdered in his cell for a large pecuniary consideration. With the butler out of the way the guilty couple did a moonlight flit and were never heard of again."

"Well, actually they were, albeit briefly," said Mrs Tucker of the *Kingsbridge Chronicle*. "On their way up to London by train they both fell to their deaths from an open carriage door. An inspector from the Great Western Railway said categorically that the door catches were in perfect working order and surmised that they were pushed out of the train. There was talk of a darkly dressed man who appeared to jump out of the train at the time of the tragedy and was not seen again.

I have researched this story because William Hutchings was my great uncle. I had always believed him guilty of the crime of arson and I thank you deeply for bringing the whole matter to light at last. I suppose that we will never know just how you found out all these new facts, not a ghost of a chance to coin a phrase…"

Miss Wilberforce

"It's very kind of you to come and look after me, young man," said Miss Wilberforce as she stood in the doorway of Acacia Cottage. She peered up at Ed, a slightly bent old lady with faded blue eyes.

Ed had known her all twenty years of his life, had grown up in the house across the lane just the other side of the wall from Miss Wilberforce's house. He had not noticed her grow old, had visited her from time to time and heard her stories of South Africa and India. He knew that she was now very old and that, despite her lisping speech and frail appearance, she had a will of iron. She had been taken for granted by all the village people for very many years, regarded as a throwback to a previous generation to whom the British Empire was everything, a shining example of progress given to less enlightened people all over the world.

"Come in now, young man. Remind me; are you Dr Crowley or Mr Kavannah, my solicitor?"

"I'm Ed and I live next door at Elm Cottage.

I've come to spend the night and make sure that you are looked after. You won't go to the Cottage Hospital for a check up and you haven't been very well just lately. I'm a medical student and my parents think that it would be a good idea if I were to sleep here when I'm home for the vacations."

"Most kind of you all I'm sure. I'll show you your bedroom, Mr Kavannah. I want you to be comfortable and I'll pay you for this of course. I'm glad you're here. I don't want my twin sister Daisy coming in here at night and taking things that are not rightfully hers. She might have been dead for years but she still has a way of making her presence felt."

"I'm sure she won't bother us tonight, or any other night for that matter. I'm glad that I'm here to take care of things."

Miss Wilberforce ushered Ed into the narrow hall and closed the front door. The house was dark and smelled musty; a mixture of coal dust and mice assailed Ed's nostrils. It was a familiar smell; Ed had been in the lower part of the house many times before.

The old lady clicked on the light in the living room. Ed saw the damask armchairs, the brick fireplace, the large print on the wall of Dr Brydon's arrival at the walls of Jellalabad on an exhausted horse, the rows of tarnished medals with their brilliant ribbons in the corner cabinet and the oil painting of a Cape Kaffir grinning over a stake fence.

Miss Wilberforce pulled heavy curtains over the darkening window panes. Outside, bats continued to flit and flicker in the warm summer air. The sinking red orb of the sun hung just above the hill across the valley and the occasional owl hooted tentatively.

"I must show you the upstairs, Dr Crowley. You will need to know where the bathroom is and where my room is. You room is at the end of the passage, just round the corner from the bathroom. Feel free to have a bath. You must be tired after examining all those patients at the Cottage Hospital. They tried to put me in there once, you know, but I wouldn't stay. I got Mrs Oldsworth to drive me home and then refused to leave. They can't make me go, you know…"

Ed noticed that the bathroom was in a wing of its own at the end of a passage between two bedrooms, one of which was Miss Wilberforce's, the other firmly shut and locked.

"One thing I must insist on, Dr Oldsworth, is that you do not, on any account, or for any reason, go into that room. I keep the door locked for very good reason. Should you trespass in that room then you will never come into this house again while I live. Do I make that quite clear?"

"Quite clear, Miss Wilberforce. Don't worry; I will do what I am told."

The old lady took his hand in her dry palm and squeezed.

"You may call me Violet and I shall call you Edward, such a manly name isn't it."

The tall young man and the bent old lady parted the best of friends. Ed made sure that she was safely tucked into her bed in her room, carefully left a chink in the curtains for her, switched off her light and bade her goodnight. He then took a bath under a dusty forty watt bulb and was glad to get between the sheets in the high wooden bed at the end of the house. He carefully folded the heavy eiderdown and put it on the upright chair in the corner of the room. Having made himself fairly comfortable on the lumpy mattress he opened a copy of M R James's *Ghost Stories of an Antiquary*, a fitting volume for the present circumstances. He knew that Miss Wilberforce slept soundly; he could hear her snores coming from down the passage. As Ed read of the stealthy approach of Count Magnus a glorious yellow moon hung above the Scots pines behind the house.

Soon Ed grew drowsy and switched off his bedside lamp. He snuggled down under the covers feeling very much at home in the house. Accompanied by Violet Wilberforce's hearty snores he drifted off to sleep with the moonlight shining in at his window. He slept well, only occasionally disturbed by a persistent scratching and thumping which seemed to come from the locked bedroom. He put it down to mice or, at worst, rats and turned luxuriantly over to fall back asleep.

He was woken in the morning by a heavy knocking at the front door. Hurriedly pulling on some clothes, Ed ran down the stairs to open the door to a lovely summer morning with the sun beaming from a cloudless sky.

On the doorstep stood a slightly younger and tidier replica of Miss Violet Wilberforce, wearing tweeds and a headscarf.

"Good morning young man, you must be Ed. I am Daisy Wilberforce, Violet's sister. Contrary to what she says I am very much alive. I have driven over to see if my sister is alright, not having heard from her for quite a number of weeks. May I come in please?"

"Of course you may, Miss Wilberforce. I will just go upstairs to tell your sister that you are here. I'm sure that she will be delighted to see you."

Daisy Wilberforce sat down on the sofa beneath the grinning kaffir, smoothing her tweed skirt over her knees. Ed mounted the curving stairs to the landing. All was quiet in Violet's bedroom. Ed thought that she must be awake by now and wondered if he should have brought her up a cup of tea.

He tapped gently on the bedroom door. There was no reply, no sound at all from Violet's room. He knocked again and called out:

"Miss Wilberforce, you have a visitor. Your sister has come to see you."

There was no sound at all from Violet's bedroom. A loud bang from the locked room startled Ed and he pushed open the door to Violet's room. His mouth fell open as he saw the dusty bed, immaculately made with sheets folded in hospital corners. No head had pressed the pillow for quite some time. No body had lain between the yellowed sheets. A few flies buzzed impotently against the clouded window panes.

"Miss Wilberforce, would you come up here please? It appears that your sister did not sleep in her bed last night. She must be in the locked room that she told me not to enter. Would you kindly open it for me please?"

Heavy steps on the stairs announced the presence of Miss Daisy. Without a word she turned the knob of the locked bedroom. The door remained fast shut. Daisy rattled the knob but could not open the door.

She looked worried.

"Put your shoulder to the door, would you?"

Ed did so without much conviction. He was most surprised when the door opened gently inward when he applied a little pressure.

The flies rose buzzing torpidly from the shrunken figure on the bed. Ed expected it to sit angrily up but was hardly surprised when it did not.

Daisy bolted gagging out of the room and crashed downstairs to find the phone.

It was obvious that Miss Violet Wilberforce had been dead for quite a number of weeks. She lay on her back with her arms at her side, her open mouth a dark void, her eyes shrunk back into her head. Ed noticed that the thin bones of her arms and legs were entirely visible through their almost transparent covering of flaking skin.

Suddenly he felt faint; who had he put to bed in the adjacent room the previous evening? He opened the window to let in the fresh summer air. There must be a rational explanation to all this, he thought desperately…

In time an explanation of sorts was forthcoming. A dusty document was found on the bedside table in the room. It proved to be a form of will. On careful reading by Mr Kavannah, it transpired that Miss Violet Wilberforce, of sound mind and reason, willed Acacia Cottage, its gardens and field, to Dr Edward Brown of Elm Cottage. All other monies and effects were to go to Miss Daisy Wilberforce, younger sister of the deceased.

Also found on the table was a check dated the day of Ed's arrival at Acacia Cottage and made out to him for the sum of nine pounds, seven shillings and fourpence.

Afterword

Ever since Pliny the Elder's account of the ghost of the murdered Athenodorus groaning and rattling his chains to lead someone to his grave in a dungheap, ghost stories have fascinated and entertained many readers over the centuries. Usually a ghost story contains a plot, a motive and a conclusion and can be a satisfying read. Sometimes, however, a ghost story can impinge on the realms of madness; no apparent motive for the haunting is offered and the denouement of the story raises more questions than can ever be answered.

Some ghosts appear rational and seek an answer from the living. Secrets can be revealed which would otherwise be lost and everyone, including the ghost, lives happily ever after. The reader is reassured that rationality continues beyond the grave and has a cosy feeling of satisfaction at the story's conclusion.

Other ghosts are the embodiment of chaos and evil. They are fuelled by a hatred that is totally unreasonable and choose as their victims random mortals with whom they have no connection except as potential victims. These are the ghosts who should be given ASBOs and never, on any account, should they be employed in hospitals, schools or in any other public institution. They are thoroughly nasty, vindictive and amoral and give their gentler cousins a bad name. You definitely disturb them at your peril.

All ghost stories contain, in lesser or greater measure, the element of guilt. A ghost is like a guilty conscience that just will not go away. The wrong done to or by the ghost grows over generations into a black hole that sucks people, connected or otherwise, into its maelstrom. There is no escape once the ghost has been summoned; no sprig of garlic or silver bullet exists to keep the monster at bay. Once the gods are challenged or offended, mortals are irredeemably doomed. "Here there be monsters!"

There is no scientific proof of the existence of ghosts, only probabilities. Thus we can set the very convincing photograph of the grey lady of Rainham Hall gliding down the staircase with arms crossed and eye sockets empty with the photograph of the Cottingley Fairies, courtesy of Pear's Soap. We would like to believe in ghosts because doing so implies the probability of some form of life after death.

Ghosts could be the returning spirits of dead people, the embodiment of the forces of good and evil, or an action replay of an historical event tuned into by certain people sensitive to atmospheres. We just don't know. If we did we probably would no longer sustain our abiding interest in, and love, of ghost stories.

Remember, Gentle Reader, that ghosts invariably produce more questions than answers.

Now to the stories, which I mainly wrote during the winter of 2006 and the spring, summer and autumn of 2007. Each is based on an actual event which took place in either Cornwall, Devon, Somerset or Dorset in the past two hundred years. I researched each story and added elements from my experience or imagination.

The first and by far the shortest, *Mr Hendra's Charabanc*, is 378 words long and won a writing competition set by *Writing Rocket*, a group of writers who organise courses in South Devon. It was published in the *Totnes Times* and is set on the evening of November 2nd, All Souls' Day, in Cornworthy in the early 1920s.

Mr Hendra is a sort of angel of death who, once a year, collects all the recently dead of the parish and removes them from the earth. No guilt here, but a compulsion to go along with one's fellow souls to wherever they are destined to go.

There was a Mr Hendra who operated a charabanc in the Totnes area between the wars. I am certain, however, that he did not have the job of transporting the dead to the afterlife. Had he done so he would have experienced bankruptcy very soon after obtaining his licence.

The second story, *A Sense of Loss*, was written after a very pleasant weekend spent at the Jamaica Inn on Bodmin Moor, when, on the Sunday morning, autumn turned to winter. In the old reception area there is a framed black and white photograph of Percy Smythe with a typewritten explanation of his disappearance. It looks very convincing and certainly had me fooled for quite a long time. However after searching on the internet and coming up with nothing, I talked to local historian Mr Peter Mullins. I read a very informative and well written book on the history of the inn by Mrs Rose Mullins and, in correspondence with her, learned that the sad framed photograph is most probably a spoof dating from the late 1940s. So Percy in reality turned out to be a figment of the imagination. Who, then, was the serious young man with the crooked smile shown in the old photograph?

I was intrigued by the date of the disappearance of the spectral Percy, the 19th January, because it was on that very date that my two youngest sons Thomas and Peter left their home in Devon to begin a new life in Florida. In this way does art imitate life.

In *Danse Macabre* I exploited a very tenuous connection between the American dancer Isadora Duncan and Kennicott House, renamed "Endicott House", the Sixth Form College of King Edward VI

Community College in Totnes, where I worked. Kennicott House was, at one time, owned by Paris Singer who was the lover of Duncan and the father of one of her unfortunate children who drowned in the River Seine when her car rolled backwards into the raging torrent. It can be said that Isadora Duncan had a lifetime of bad luck with cars.

The photograph, however, is genuine and suggests a tall female figure with a long scarf. Kennicott House has a few "cold spots" and something nasty in the cellar. Ask any of the caretakers or staff who worked there when the house was the former boarding house for the boys' grammar school. Recently some grainy footage of Isadora dancing on the lawn of Kennicott House has come to light.

The Old A38 exploits a very well known Westcountry urban (or rather rural) myth. There has been much research on the legendary white-mackintoshed man who waves his dry thumb at hapless motorists on rainy days. I have met a man, a friend of my father's, who has seen the phantom hitchhiker. Here, in the story, is an example of a misunderstood ghost who looks horrible but is well intentioned, even though his stories are not always in the best possible taste. He delivers just a hint of gratuitous nastiness but redeems himself in the end.

Room Number 4 refers to a room in the White Hart Hotel in Launceston which, I am reliably informed by a member of staff, has a strange atmosphere. There is not a jot of evidence that Mr Hardy, commercial traveller of Worcester and carrier of cholera, spent his last night on earth in that actual room, but it is a matter of record that he died of that fell disease in one of the rooms at the White Hart and that he did not emerge or let himself be contacted until after his death. Because of his selfless action, cholera did not stalk the streets of Launceston. Mr Hardy was buried in a lead lined coffin and the bells of St Mary Magdalene were rung at his funeral in thanks for the deliverance of the town from pestilence. Mr Hardy's monument can be seen near the south door of the church of St Mary Magdalene in Launceston. A masterpiece of Victorian understatement, it makes no mention of cholera, merely stating that John Hardy, commercial traveller of Worcester, aged thirty-nine, died in Launceston while there on business.

The Mr Ching visited by Mr Hardy's dutiful and industrious ghost was four times mayor of Launceston, a successful businessman and innovator and brother of Thomas Prockter Ching who went to sea in the barque *Charles Eaton* to be stranded on the uncharted Great Barrier Reef off the coast of Australia in August 1834. After many desperate adventures he was rescued by Torres Strait islanders who killed and ate him and most of his companions on the tiny island of Boydong. I tell his story and that of the few survivors in my novel *A Hollow Sea*. Thomas Ching's plain monument can be found not far from Mr Hardy's in St Mary Magdalene's church in Launceston.

Launceston is a wonderful hilltop Cornish town just a stone's throw from the border with Devon. Ching's house is now Mr Hicks' drapery shop a couple of doors away from the White Hart Inn. The town is well worth a visit with its castle, winding streets and extensive views of the surrounding countryside. It is one of my favourite small towns anywhere.

The next story, *Tom Tucker,* comes from my ten years as a volunteer on the South Devon Railway, a steam railway run in true great Western tradition between Buckfastleigh and Totnes in South Devon. I graduated from booking clerk to guard on the line and very much enjoyed writing this story. At last we have a thoroughly nasty ghost who doesn't care who he harms in his quest for revenge. There was an unfortunate fireman who hanged himself in Ashburton engine shed early one Victorian morning. There was also a one-legged crossing keeper at Knapper's Crossing near Staverton who lived in the cottage near the line. His name was not Narramore but James and he did not harbour a grudge against immediate members of his family. I write this in the hope that I am correct and that I will not be visited by a one-legged ghost!

Operation Paper Tiger takes me back to my days as a trooper in D Squadron, Royal Devon Yeomanry, Royal Armoured Corps, Territorial Army. The imaginary exercise takes place on the fortieth anniversary of the disastrous practice landings on Slapton and Blackpool Sands. Nearly one thousand American soldiers and sailors lost their lives in live firing exercises and in the sinking of assault ships in Lyme Bay. Among them was a very distant cousin, Specialist Four Clarence Van Nostrand.

Sergeant Black's reconnaissance patrol finds itself in a time warp with its radio batteries drained and absolutely no contact with the rest of the exercise. The soldiers encounter a group of spectral American soldiers who are as frightened and as bewildered as themselves.

I have heard from two reliable first hand witnesses that the American dead were buried, temporarily at least, in a field directly opposite the Forces Inn on the Totnes to Dartmouth road. Although the name of the pub reflects the happenings of Operation Tiger, its name has an older and more sinister meaning. "Forches" were originally "gallows" and were often situated at a crossroads, as is the case with the modern day Forces Inn.

The ghost of *Veyther* (Father) is gratuitously malignant and just didn't like being disturbed. He was a disaster waiting to happen and it didn't matter a jot to him that his victim was a decent man who held no grudge against anyone. The story of "Zaltin' down Veyther against the spring" is well known and probably happened at the old Warren House Inn which lay just across the road from the present establishment.

The Inn is even more rugged and isolated than its Cornish cousin the Jamaica Inn. It is one of the highest inns in the country and is well worth a visit, especially in winter when coach loads of tourists are notably absent. It has a fire in the bar which has reputedly burned continuously for hundreds of years. It is said that when the new inn was built during the early years of Queen Victoria's reign, the fire was transferred over the road from the old inn on a shovel.

In the late 1920s the landlord did fatally shoot himself behind the bar at closing time. I would like to think that he could not have borne the prospect of another night in the lonely inn with the unspeakable "Veyther".

Some of the most terrifying ghosts are those phantoms you cannot get away from in the open air. The undead creature that came after Crane in the fastnesses of the central moor could not be avoided, outpaced or hidden from. Crane's last moments were the ultimate paranoia.

"Veyther" might have been a nameless spectre but *John "Babbacombe" Lee* was a very real person with a very real story which he told in countless Devon pubs until his death from old age. His doleful features were photographically recorded on numerous occasions. He did indeed cheat the hangman, possibly in the way that I have suggested. He served over twenty years in various prisons before returning home to Abbotskerswell, from which village he moved away to the Tavistock area. His ghost is obviously a vengeful one: poor Gerald survived the accident on the M5 only possibly to die alone at home at the hands of a homicidal spook.

Floreat Totnesia is the old school song of the former King Edward VI Grammar School in Totnes. The youths depicted in this story are thinly disguised friends and contemporaries of mine from my sixth form days of forty years ago. I will not bore you by identifying them. The legends discussed in the story are well known, as is Robert Graves' unpleasant experience at Berry Pomeroy Castle.

At the end of each academic year I organise a walk from Totnes to Berry Pomeroy Castle and back on old trackways and green lanes. It is this route that I describe in the story. Once again we encounter a disaster waiting to happen, a slow-release doom stretching over several decades. I am glad to say that, to the best of my knowledge, all my friends in the story are all in rude health at the moment.

A very strange thing happened to me while writing this story. I was just completing the paragraph in which the ghostly lady appears on the ramparts when my computer screen turned completely blank. Instead of ordered lines of words there was a ghastly milky whiteness. Twenty one thousand carefully written words had vanished into the void to be lost for eternity.

Fortunately I had the whole document in hard copy and my network manager son was able to scan it back to me so that I could reformat it and restore it to the internal ether of my ageing computer. The moral of this tale is that if you forget how to store a document on a CD the ghost in the machine will get you sooner or later.

In writing *Private Angove* I took a great liberty with the honourable history of the Duke of Cornwall's Light Infantry. As far as I am aware no DCLI soldier was shot for cowardice or desertion during the course of World War I. I hope that I will be able to continue to visit the excellent DCLI museum in Bodmin without being arrested and clapped in irons. I realise that Private Angove was, in fact, no coward but a man shell-shocked beyond all human endurance.

There is a connection between Angove and his former home *Chy an Gof* which becomes obvious with a little study of the Cornish language. *An Gof* in Cornish (*Le Goff* in Breton) is a blacksmith. Angove is the anglicised form of the word; he was really

Private Smith, a Cornish representative of the many unfortunate victims of "the War to End All Wars".

In the garden of my house in the village of Ashprington, near Totnes in south Devon, I have found quite a large number of Army buttons and badges from the First World War. The buttons range from the Devonshire Regiment and the Royal Marine Light Infantry (actually a Navy button) to numerous general service buttons. I have a Staffordshire Regiment collar dog and a Devonshire Regiment shoulder title. It is most unlikely that anyone would ever find a complete set of buttons and badges unless directed to do so by a ghost.

Young Harry was a story that virtually wrote itself. I recently visited the much improved Bodmin Gaol where I researched the sad story of Selina Wadge of Altarnun and her execution at the gaol for infanticide. All the events in the story actually happened apart from the supposition that Selina's baby was the son of Satan, or "Old Harry". Mr Dewer, the child's imaginary father, had a surname derived from an old Devon name for the Devil. In truth the child did have deformed feet and was unable to walk, a fate that would befall anyone with cloven hooves.

The name Selina fits very well with the story, being derived from Selene the moon goddess. Selena Wadge was the last woman to be hanged in Cornwall.

As a footnote it is interesting to note that the Dr Quiller-Couch who was physician to Bodmin Gaol at the time of Selina Wadge's execution was the father of Sir Arthur Quiller-Couch the Oxford scholar, writer and critic who was born in Bodmin and who later lived for years in Fowey. 'Q' wrote many novels and some striking ghost stories. It was in company with his daughter Foy that Daphne du Maurier went riding on Bodmin Moor (once known as Fowey Moor), was hopelessly lost in the fog and was brought by her horse to the Jamaica Inn at Bolventor. The result of this nearly disastrous adventure was the writing of the novel *Jamaica Inn*.

I have always had a great dislike of *Sir Cloudesley Shovell* which is quite probably misplaced. He did hang the seaman who dared to suggest that his navigation was at fault. In Sir Cloudesley's defence is the fact that, in the reign of Queen Anne, it was nearly impossible to calculate a ship's longitude in the absence of a reliable chronometer. It was Mr Harrison who perfected the timepiece and probably saved many subsequent ships from running aground. Having said that, I must admit that the ship's chronometer on my dining room wall loses an average of five minutes a week.

There is no evidence that the woman who killed Sir Cloudesley as he lay on the beach on St Mary's had any connection with the Scillonian sailor hanged on the *Association*. An old lady did confess to this act on her deathbed and handed over one of the Rear Admiral's rings.

Vade Mecum (Come with me) is a rather fanciful account of how I was inspired to write my historical novel *A Hollow Sea*. Ching's ghost is a gentle one who definitely has a story worth telling.

Cutty Dyer is the name of a troll who is rumoured to lurk under the hump-backed bridge over the River Yeo in Kingsbridge Lane in the very pleasant town of Ashburton. The doggerel rhyme is well known in books of Devon folklore. Whether Cutty is a folk memory of a particularly nasty man who used to hurl people into the river or a sinister elemental spirit only those who have met him and survived can tell.

T.E.Lawrence served as a private soldier in the Royal Tank Regiment until his untimely death in 1935. He kept a little cottage at *Clouds Hill* as an escape from service life. It is now owned by the National Trust and open to the public. There are reports that his ghost has been seen at the remote little house dressed in Arab robes.

There are lots of conspiracy theories that various political groups had him killed in the road accident described in the story. My feeling is that they are probably unfounded; T.E. was a notoriously fast and reckless driver. I recently met a lady in Torquay whose nephew was one of the boys who witnessed the accident. Apparently T.E.Lawrence roundly cursed the three boys who had caused him to come to grief before lapsing into a coma. It remains a great pity that his life was suddenly cut short when he was in his mid forties.

On the granite arch at the entrance to Dartmoor Prison in the remote and lofty village of Princetown are engraved the words *Parcere Subjectis* (Spare the Vanquished) which remind us that the prison was built in the late eighteen century to accommodate French prisoners of the Napoleonic War. Its use as a convict prison came much later.

It is true that the three named soldiers died of exposure on the moor in the middle of the nineteenth century. There is a monument to them in the church of St Michael in Princetown and another on the wall of the churchyard. The church is well worth a visit, being the only church in England built by French prisoners and fitted out by American naval prisoners of the War of 1812. At the moment the church is being skilfully and enthusiastically restored. You might find it a chilling place, especially in winter. It has no heating.

In *An Adventure* I unashamedly take the title from the celebrated book written by Miss Moberly and Miss Jordain in which they relate their experiences in the grounds of the Palace of Versailles which took place in 1901. They claim to have been transported back in time to July of 1789 when the French monarchy was forced to flee from their power base when they heard news that the revolutionary mob was approaching from Paris. So convincing was the ladies' story that their map drawn from memory of the gardens was later proved accurate by the discovery of plans signed by the king which were hidden in the chimney of a house during the Revolution and discovered after the book was written.

There is no evidence that the two ladies ever visited Lyme Regis. Had they done so it is quite probable that one of them could have re-lived the landslip that happened in 1839. If one can go back in time then, consequently, one should be able to go forward and find out the outcome of an event that is happening in the present.

Mrs Carey - Carew is not only a guilty wraith but also a malevolent one. She is unable to rest until her secret is found out and she is equally unwilling for that to happen. Schizophrenic ghosts can be the most dangerous; their minds are divided and their intentions confused.

The ghostly howl which seemed to come from all around rather than from one specific place is something that I experienced at the age of eleven. At the time I attended a private school at Loventor Manor near Berry Pomeroy. The school was situated at the end of a long drive about half a mile from Berry

Pomeroy Castle, whose ragged walls could be clearly seen on their crag during the winter months.

The house was mainly Georgian with Tudor kitchens and apartments at the back. Something haunted Loventor Manor and made its presence felt one Friday afternoon by howling and moaning and by roughly pushing my sister to the ground. The legend is that the house had been the headquarters of a notorious female highwayman who robbed coaches on the Newton Abbot and on the Paignton roads before being hanged from an ancient oak tree at nearby Glazegate Cross on the present Berry Pomeroy to Marldon road. There might be some truth in this legend as the name "Glazegate" is a contraction of "Gallows Gate". The isolated crossroads is still known to locals as "Hangman's Cross".

I have never been privileged to actually see a ghost, but I have felt a malevolent presence. Twice I have entered the ancient church of St Paul de Leon at Staverton in south Devon to experience a sudden drop in temperature and the eerie feeling of being watched from a point somewhere near the screen. On the first occasion I was forced to leave the church to warm myself in the sunshine and to escape the evil scrutiny. On subsequent occasions I have been aware of the presence but have been able to remain inside the church. It is curious to note that, at the time, the vicar of Staverton was related to me by marriage.

The next story *It wasn't William* came to me as a result of some work I did at Hendham House near Woodleigh, deep in the South Hams of Devon overlooking the wooded valley of the River Avon. The owner of the house told me that the ghost of a girl had been seen over the years in on of the rooms in the top storey of the house. Her name was Sarah and she had probably been a servant in the house. Today she is no longer there. Her message had been that "It wasn't William…"

I made up all the rest, taking the name of the owners who burned the house down as "Nicholls". This was a cheap trick; the owners of a nearby house, Oldstone House near Blackawton, was "Dimes". They are reputed to have burned their house down for the insurance money and are supposed to have been imprisoned for it at the turn of the twentieth century. Today the remains of the house can be seen in a farmyard near the main Totnes-Dartmouth road. I am glad to say that Hendham House has never had a fire and is a peaceful place of great beauty.

If you visit the Woodland Leisure Park near Oldstone House you will see the pond in which a Victorian member of the Dimes family was found floating upright but dead, presumably murdered by her husband who escaped abroad soon after the deed. There should be a ghost story in that…

The last story, *Miss Wilberforce,* takes place in Ashprington, the Devon village in which I have lived, on and off, for the last fifty two years. When I was a student I used to sleep at the house next door to keep an eye on an old lady who, despite failing health, insisted on living alone. The description of the house is exact; the difference between the story and reality is that the house definitely was not haunted. I always knew that the old lady was alive by her stentorian snoring which often kept me awake.

So there you have it; twenty one ghost stories ranging from the mild to the downright nasty. They are certainly not to be taken too seriously but should be treated as entertaining fantasies.

Or are we whistling in the dark? The uneasy spirits of the restless dead are somewhere out there beyond the firelight and the heavy curtains. They cannot be denied: I leave you with one of the most disturbing verses of the terrifying lyrical ballad *The Rime of the Ancient Mariner* by the Devonian poet Samuel Taylor Coleridge who leaves us:

Like one, that on a lonesome road
Doth walk in fear and dread,
And having once turned round, walks on
And turns no more his head;
Because he knows a frightful fiend
Doth close behind him tread.

Notes

These pages are for the reader to make notes about
the stories or the locations visited.

Notes

Blackstone's
Police Q&A

Crime 2023